Sam picked up one of Becky's crayons and held his hand out to Kayla.

"How do you sign *blue?*" he asked, looking directly at her.

Kayla glanced down. "That's not a blue crayon."

"I was talking about your eyes. They're very blue...and your cheeks are suddenly bright pink." Sam smiled and leaned closer. "I can learn *all* my colors," he murmured, "just by looking at you."

Kayla's heart thumped.

"There are more signs than just colors, you know."

"True." Sam smiled again. "So, how do you say *I?*"

Kayla pointed her index finger at herself.

"And how do you say *want?*"

Kayla hesitated then held both palms up and crooked her fingers as she pulled her hands toward her body.

Sam leaned even closer.

"And how do you say *a kiss?*" he whispered against her ear.

Dear Reader,

I love putting characters into situations they don't know how to handle! A "fish out of water" story usually means a character is taken from his or her everyday surroundings and plopped down in a new location. In *A Rancher's Pride*, the opposite has happened with heart-wrenching results.

Ranch owner Sam Robertson becomes an instant daddy when—without a breath of warning—his ex-wife gives him the care of his four-year-old daughter, Becky. Sam has his hands full just learning to deal with a child. But his situation is even more challenging because Becky is deaf and he doesn't know how to communicate with her.

I'll admit, in this book, I tortured my hero. Though Sam is a fumbling father, he's determined to do what's right for his child. Then, in comes the heroine. Becky's aunt, Kayla Ward, has all the skills Sam lacks. She also has plans to take his little girl away from him....

Writing *A Rancher's Pride* kept me on the verge of tears, because even *I* wasn't sure how Sam, Kayla and Becky could ever reach a happy ending.

I would love to hear what you think about this story. You can reach me at P.O. Box 504, Gilbert, AZ 85299 or through my website: www.barbarawhitedaille.com. I'm also on Facebook: www.facebook.com/barbarawhitedaille and Twitter: twitter.com/BarbaraWDaille.

All my best to you!

Until we meet again,

Barbara White Daille

A Rancher's Pride
BARBARA WHITE DAILLE

TORONTO NEW YORK LONDON
AMSTERDAM PARIS SYDNEY HAMBURG
STOCKHOLM ATHENS TOKYO MILAN MADRID
PRAGUE WARSAW BUDAPEST AUCKLAND

Recycling programs
for this product may
not exist in your area.

ISBN-13: 978-0-373-75357-4

A RANCHER'S PRIDE

Copyright © 2011 by Barbara White-Rayczek

www.Harlequin.com

Printed in U.S.A.

ABOUT THE AUTHOR

Barbara White Daille lives with her husband in the sunny Southwest, where they don't mind the lizards in their front yard but could do without the scorpions in the bathroom.

A writer from the age of nine and a novelist since eighth grade, Barbara is now an award-winning author with a number of novels to her credit.

When she was very young, Barbara learned from her mom about the storytelling magic in books—and she's been hooked ever since. She hopes you will enjoy reading her books and will find your own magic in them!

Books by Barbara White Daille

HARLEQUIN AMERICAN ROMANCE
1131—THE SHERIFF'S SON
1140—COURT ME, COWBOY
1328—FAMILY MATTERS

To Judy
for cowboys and ranchers,
long lunches and laughter,
and for always believing,
and of course, to Rich

Chapter One

The minute Sam Robertson saw his mother's frozen expression, he knew something terrible had happened. He hadn't seen that look on Sharleen's face since the night his daddy died.

He tossed his Stetson onto the hook by the kitchen door and crossed the room to where she sat at the table. The mouthwatering smell of beef and vegetables came from a bubbling pot of stew on the stove. He was home later than normal, but the table wasn't yet set for their supper. "Mom? What is it? What's wrong?"

She shook her head for a second, as if she couldn't speak. Lines crinkled the skin around her blue eyes. She looked about ten years older than when he'd left for the north pasture early that morning.

"What's going on?" he asked.

"Sam…" She cleared her throat and started again. "Ronnie was here."

"Ronnie?" He frowned. He hadn't seen his ex-wife in five years. If things had worked the way he wanted, he'd have never heard her name again. "What did she want after all this time? Just stopping by to say hello?"

"She said she's settling down again. With another man."

"That's what has you upset? You should know better."

Sam laughed shortly. "And we should both pity the poor guy. So, what did she do, come all the way from Chicago to drop off an invitation to the wedding?"

"No." Sharleen brushed her fingertips across the hair near her temple.

A nervous gesture he hadn't seen, either, since the months right after his daddy's death. Whatever the news, she didn't know how to cope with telling him. How bad could it be? He'd written his ex out of his life a long time ago. She couldn't do anything to affect him.

He sank into the chair beside hers. "Come on. Just let me have it. What did she want?"

Sharleen took a deep breath and let it out slowly. Finally, she said, "She dropped something off, but not an invitation. She brought a little girl with her. Four years old. Ronnie left her here. She said she's your daughter."

"What?" The news rocked him back in the chair. "That's impossible."

"I'm not sure that it is."

He stared at her.

"The child is blonde," she continued. "Like Ronnie. But she's got your eyes. Your daddy's eyes. She looks like a Robertson, through and through." She waved toward the arched doorway. "See for yourself."

After a moment's hesitation, he rose and moved to the door. He had to brace himself before he could step into the living room.

Everything looked familiar. The pair of plaid couches facing each other. The long pine coffee table between them. The clock ticking away on the mantel. Everything looked familiar, except the child sitting on one of the couches.

A beautiful little girl.

The daughter he'd always hoped for, the start of the family he'd never had.

He shook his head. Pipe dreams, for sure. Ronnie had never told a true story in her life. This child couldn't be his.

She wore a blue T-shirt, white shorts and denim sneakers. In her arms, she cradled a stuffed tiger. A couple of dolls rested on the couch alongside her.

As he moved another step into the room, she looked up.

Small and blonde, just as Sharleen had said. And more.

The girl's eyes shone in the light from the table lamp beside the couch. Silver-gray eyes surrounded by dark lashes, a perfect match to his own.

His throat tightened. He felt frozen in place.

She gave him a shy smile.

He'd seen that half-twisted grin in plenty of his own childhood pictures. Not impossible after all. The child was his.

Somehow, after what seemed like hours, he managed to raise one hand to wave at her. "Hello." The word came out in a croak. He hadn't the first idea of what to say and went for the standard opening line. "What's your name?"

Sharleen moved up to stand behind him and rested her hand on his arm. "Her name's Becky," she told him. "But she can't hear you, Sam. She's deaf."

FROM THE SHADOWS OF THE BARN doorway the next afternoon, Sam stole a glance across the yard to where his little girl played by the back porch steps, unmindful of anything near her.

If he had reason to yell Becky's name, she wouldn't

hear him. If Porter's uncontrollable mutt appeared from the ranch next door and made a beeline for her, she wouldn't know. If the house collapsed behind her, she'd never have a clue—unless she saw the dust cloud kicked up from the falling debris.

And, worst of all, Sam couldn't explain any of this to her.

He couldn't communicate with his daughter at all.

Jack, his ranch foreman, nodded in Becky's direction. "Look at her, boss. The girl's taking things in stride."

"Better than I am."

Jack shrugged. "Not every day a man's ex saddles him with a kid he's not expecting."

"Well, I have her now." His gut tightened every time he recalled Sharleen's story of how Ronnie had breezed in and hustled out of the ranch house, waving an over-the-shoulder goodbye as if she'd done no more than deliver a mail-order package. What made her do it, after all this time…? He couldn't hazard a guess. Maybe her soon-to-be husband had a say in the matter.

"Sharleen's handling things, too," Jack said.

"Yeah. But neither of us is going to be able to cope with a child who can't talk. Besides, my mother's getting up there, and a four-year-old's more than she can handle." Especially this one.

Late-afternoon sunbeams slanted through the cedar trees edging the yard. Becky ran from a patch of darkness into light and back again, playing her private, silent game. As they watched, she stumbled. Sam slapped his hand flat against the wooden barn door. If she hurt herself, how would he comfort her?

Geez. Talk about overreacting.

Or was it?

Could he ever keep Becky safe?

His breath caught in a half-strangled hitch. "Damn," he muttered. "What in hell am I going to do?"

"Take care of the kid," Jack said.

Like it was that easy.

Becky settled on the grass and began tugging on a few of the yellow dandelions Sam never had time to weed. Safe enough for her there. For the moment.

Take care of her.

Right.

Looking out across the yard, he said, "Laying in fence, breaking a horse, rounding up cattle. Jack, those jobs, you know I can handle with my eyes closed."

The foreman nodded.

"But this…" How could he take care of a deaf four-year-old daughter he hadn't, till yesterday, even known existed?

Raising his gaze, he looked as far as he could see, focusing on the higher pastures and, above them, the ranks of piñon and pine. Viewing the extent of his ranch usually gave him pleasure, but right now, even that sight couldn't take him from his troubles.

"Sam." Jack pointed.

From down the road a ways, a shiny blue four-door sedan neared the house. The driver pulled in at the front of the property and climbed out, then slammed the door closed behind her.

Jack whistled, long and low.

Sam nodded, unsmiling. His ex had soured him on women years ago. Though he'd finally started thinking about the sweeter side of them again, Ronnie's visit had sure put paid to any good thoughts about the so-called fairer sex.

What she'd done hadn't been fair at all.

To him and Sharleen. Or to Becky.

The woman in the driveway wore a bright pink T-shirt. A skimpy cotton jacket and a brand-new pair of jeans called attention to curves that even stiff denim couldn't hide.

Sam gave himself a mental shake. You'd think he hadn't seen a woman since his divorce. Heck, he had plenty of female friends—even if a good number of them had reached the age to collect their retirement pay.

"Man," Jack said, "if that's new hired help, she can help me out anytime."

Sam frowned. "I don't know who she is."

He took one last look at Becky. She had climbed onto the wooden swing at the far side of the back porch, well out of sight of anyone out at the road. Sharleen stood nearby taking windblown sheets off the line.

He crossed the yard and headed toward the front of the house at a lope, taking in the woman as he neared her. She looked even better close up. Long, golden-brown hair the color of honey pine. Eyes the blue of a lake in winter. And those curves. *Whoa.*

He'd never seen a vision like this one before, and he knew every soul in Flagman's Folly.

"I'm Sam Robertson. What can I do for you?"

As she looked at him, those blue eyes froze over.

A warning bell rang somewhere deep in his memory. "Don't I know you?"

"You should. I'm Kayla Ward."

"As in Ronnie Ward?"

She nodded. "I'm her sister. You don't recognize me?"

He looked closer. His insides tightened and his pulse picked up. Yeah, he remembered her now, no matter how briefly he'd seen her the first time they'd crossed paths.

He *should* have known her instantly. The one and only time he'd seen her had been branded into his mind. But back then, her face hadn't mattered to him. It was her actions that had rocked him. That had stuck with him through the years. She had helped Ronnie pack up and head out. Had walked off with his wife and—if only he'd known it—his daughter.

It would be just like his ex to send her here again, claiming she'd changed her mind about Becky.

Well, if this woman thought she'd waltz in here and take his daughter away, she had another think coming.

"What do you want?" he demanded.

She glanced past him toward Jack and the barn. "Can we talk inside?"

He opened his mouth to snap a negative reply, then shut it again. Aware that Becky played just around the corner, he nodded. Better not to let this woman get anywhere near her.

He gestured for Kayla to go ahead of him.

Inside the house, he had to clear their path of a couple of pillows left on the living room floor. He tossed them onto the couch. With Becky around, already he'd noticed the changes in the orderliness of this place. And of his life.

As for the woman in front of him…

Well, he'd take care of this situation the same way he dealt with trouble on the ranch—one crisis at a time. Only, lately, it seemed the catastrophes had a way of piling up.

"What do you want?" he repeated.

"I want Becky."

He nodded. "That figures. Ronnie sent you, right? She changed her mind already?" He laughed scornfully. "She dumped Becky off on me, in case you didn't know."

"I do know." She reached up, slicked a hank of hair behind her ear, then clasped her hands together. Every move made it obvious she was gearing up for something. "I'm here to bring Becky home again."

"You—" In spite of knowing what she had to be up to, the words hit him hard. He glared down at her, his jaw clenched tight. It took effort to speak, and he didn't bother to keep his tone civil. "Not gonna happen."

No one would ever take his daughter from him again.

"You can't keep her here—"

His harsh laugh cut her off midsentence. "The hell I can't. Did Ronnie forget to tell you? Or just feed you another one of her lies? She gave me sole custody of Becky."

A strangled sound came from her, as if someone had gut-punched every ounce of air from her lungs.

"You didn't know about that, did you?"

For a second, he might've felt sorry for her, the way she believed in her scheming sister. But the thought of what Kayla had come here planning to do—and the reminder of what she *had* done to him five years ago— drove all pity from him. "Ronnie will never walk out of here with Becky again. Neither will you."

"I don't believe you. Ronnie told me—"

"Ronnie told you wrong. I've got an appointment with the judge in town tomorrow morning. You could come and find out—except you're not going to be here that long."

Kayla Ward stared at him without saying a word,

which came as a surprise. Somehow, she didn't seem the type to give in that easily.

Another look at her face—eyes cold and homed in on him—proved him right. She hadn't given in at all.

She moved closer. Near enough that he could smell whatever she used in her hair, some kind of shampoo that made him think of wildflowers and sweet grass.

"Becky hasn't even been here twenty-four hours yet," she said.

"Long enough for you to have gotten here five times over, if you were all that concerned."

"I was out of town at a conference," she protested. "I didn't know what had happened until I got home this morning. Then I took the next flight out." She stopped, shook her head. "What does that matter? The point is, I want to take Becky back home. Why would you want her here?" She glared at him. "You don't even know each other."

"She's my daughter."

"Does *she* know that?"

He frowned, taken aback. "What do you mean?"

"Have you told her you're her daddy? Did she understand you?" She took a deep breath and blinked rapidly, probably to hide the moisture he'd seen suddenly brightening her eyes. "I'm sure you weren't ever expecting to have the responsibility for your daughter. Since Ronnie 'dumped Becky off' here, as you called it, I assume you're saying she didn't give you any notice. She's left Becky unannounced at my mom and dad's house plenty of times over the years, too."

"Well, you can tell your folks they don't need to worry about that anymore."

"I don't have to tell them anything. I'm bringing their granddaughter home with me."

"Like hell—" The sounds of sneakers slap-slapping on the pine floor made him break off and stare over her shoulder.

From the archway connecting the kitchen and living room, Becky burst into the room. She gave a high-pitched shriek and broke into a grin.

Kayla whirled away from him. As Becky flung herself forward, Kayla opened her arms wide. The force of their meeting nearly rocked the woman back on her heels. Sam put his hands out to steady her, but she caught her balance on her own. As he watched, she hugged Becky, let go, and started gesturing in the air in front of her.

Becky's little arms waved in response.

While the exchange went on, Sam stood motionless.

Becky gave another high-pitched yelp and moved away to run into the kitchen again.

Kayla turned to him. "Becky went to get her dolls," she said in an expressionless tone. "Like any four-year-old, she wants to show off her toys." She folded her arms across her chest. "But you don't know that, do you? You couldn't understand a word we were saying."

Before he could blurt out the heated response that shot into his mind, Becky reappeared in the doorway. Behind her, she pulled along her doll-filled wagon. At least Ronnie had heart enough to leave the kid with some toys.

His heart lurched at the sight of the cart. A feeling of warmth spread through him. He'd kept that wagon upstairs in an extra bedroom, never knowing whether a child of his would ever play with it. She sure seemed attached to the thing.

She parked the wagon at the end of the sofa. Then she turned to her aunt, brought the fingertips of each hand together in a small circle and tapped her hands against each other.

"More," Kayla informed him.

He said nothing.

Becky ran across the living room and up the stairs to the second floor.

"She signed *more*," Kayla explained. "But you didn't understand that, either." Her voice trembled. "It's ridiculous to think you can keep Becky here when you can't even talk with her."

His heart bucked as if she'd spurred him. Not bothering to soften his action or his words, he leaned toward her. "Yeah? If you're so good, why didn't Ronnie leave her with you?" That shut her up. "Give me a break. Becky's been here less than a day—as you pointed out yourself. Besides, I'm her daddy and I've got custody of her now. You've got no say in the matter." He gritted his teeth and stabbed a finger toward the entryway. "There's the door. Use it."

"I'm not leav—"

A loud bang cut her off.

His thoughts flew to Becky before his mind recognized the slamming of the back door. The sound of heavy footsteps thudded across the kitchen floor.

Jack appeared in the archway, his face tight with strain. "Sam. Sharleen—she's had a fall out in the yard. It looks bad. I've already called for an ambulance."

Sam froze, staring across to the other side of the room.

Becky came down the stairs again, a doll held in either arm. Seeing all three adults looking at her, she froze, too, her brows creased in a frown. She looked at her aunt.

Kayla gestured quickly to her, then said to Sam, "Go. Do what you have to do. I'll be here with Becky."

He didn't move.

"It's all right," she urged. "Becky knows me—you saw that. She trusts me. Just go."

In the two seconds Sam stood there, Kayla's rapid hand movements left Becky with a smile on her face. Still torn, Sam hurried to follow Jack outside. Across the yard, he could see Sharleen lying on the ground, propped up on her elbows.

Even before they'd reached her, he knew the ranch manager was right; if she hadn't been able to get to her feet, things couldn't be good. His heart thumped heavily as he raced to his mother's side.

"It's okay," he said, kneeling in the dirt beside her. "Help's on the way. Hear it?"

From the county road came the swelling shriek of a siren, something they hardly ever heard this far out from town. By the sound, it wouldn't take the ambulance long to get here. That rapidly approaching blare was one of the most welcome noises Sam had heard in a while.

"I'll handle things here," he murmured to Jack. "You do something to corral that woman's car."

Jack's brows shot up.

"Tell you later," Sam said tersely.

He nodded. "You got it, boss."

"And check on them in the house once in a while."

Sam exhaled heavily. Not a good idea, leaving Becky alone with that woman. But what choice did he have? All his ranch hands were out working yet, and Jack had an arm's-length list of chores that had to be done before sundown. No time for him to watch a little girl.

And a hospital emergency room, from late in the

afternoon until who knew what time they'd get out of there, was no place for that little girl, either.

He hoped Jack hurried with his task.

Becky might believe in her aunt, but Sam didn't have a lick of confidence in Kayla. No way would he fall for her playing the trust card.

No way would he give her the chance to run off with his daughter. Again.

Chapter Two

Kayla's cell phone rang, startling her. As she bolted upright on the couch and grabbed her shoulder bag, the mantel clock gently chimed the hour. Ten. Becky had been asleep since eight.

Sam had been gone nearly four hours.

Fuzzy-headed, Kayla dug in her bag for the phone. She must have dropped off about twenty minutes ago.

The quiet had unnerved her. Back home, there was always some type of noise in the neighborhood, even this late. Car horns, traffic, someone's television blaring canned laughter into the night.

In Sam's living room, there were only the sounds of the clock ticking and a little girl's rhythmic breathing.

And the phone.

Finally she found it and flipped it open. Even half-asleep, she recognized the Chicago number. "Hello?"

"Kayla. Matt Lawrence."

Matt, the husband of one of the teachers she worked with, was a good friend. Even more, he was a tough-fighting attorney who would lend a hand to anyone in trouble, in a heartbeat. "Thanks for getting back to me. I'm sorry to bother you and Kerry this late."

"No problem. She told me you said to call no matter what time. What's up?"

"It's bad news. And I need your help." Briefly, she filled him in on what she had learned such a short time before.

"And Ronnie just went off and left Becky?" He sounded shocked. "When was this?"

"Yesterday. But we didn't find out until this morning—she'd left a message on my parents' answering machine saying she would be out of town for a while and had brought Becky to her ex."

Her mother had come into the living room from the kitchen, stunned after hearing the message.

Though Kayla had just arrived home from her conference, she immediately turned and raced back to O'Hare and jumped on the next flight to New Mexico, her mind consumed by one thought only—finding her niece.

She glanced over to where Becky lay sleeping on the couch, one doll tucked in on either side of her, the rest sitting in her charming Old West wagon.

How could Ronnie have brought her child to Sam after all this time? And why would she? Kayla could still recall the fear in her sister's voice when she had called five years ago, begging for help to pack up her belongings and get away from the ranch. Away from Sam.

Just as they had started down the road, he had come out of the barn. Kayla had felt compelled to risk one glance over her shoulder. She'd wished ever since that she hadn't looked back. The expression on Sam's face had stayed with her all this time, too.

Roughly, she pushed the memories away.

Once she tracked Ronnie down, she would find out what had possessed her to leave Becky here.

"Where are you?" Matt asked.

"In New Mexico. Here with Becky. At her…her father's house."

"He's there with you? Can you talk freely?"

"No, he's not here. We're alone." She recounted what had happened since her arrival at the ranch, including Sam's threat of a meeting with the judge the next morning. Simply repeating the words aloud made her shudder. She closed her eyes, trying not to groan.

"Matt, he *can't* get custody. He hasn't had contact with Becky—*or* Ronnie—since the day she was born. But his mother claims Ronnie verbally gave Sam custody. What if the judge backs that up? What can I do?" She fought to keep her voice from rising.

"Listen to me, Kayla," he said calmly. "What you can't do is anything to make the situation worse than it is already. Don't try to take the child anywhere until we get this checked out. Especially across state lines, or you'll be facing serious charges you won't be able to avoid. Do you understand what I'm saying?"

"Yes," she said, wincing. The idea of fleeing with Becky had already occurred to her. Whether or not she would have followed through on kidnapping her own niece, she had no way of knowing—thanks to Sam Robertson's trick with her rental car. "Don't worry, I'm not going anywhere."

"I'll see what I can do about putting a trace on Ronnie. Do you want me to do a background check on Robertson?"

Of course she did. Whatever she needed to do to take Becky home with her, she would do. Still, she hesitated. Did she have the right to open Ronnie's secrets to everyone? Maybe that wouldn't be necessary. "Hold off on the check, Matt. Let's see what happens tomorrow."

"Are you planning to appear in court with him?"

"You bet I am."

"Good." He paused, then added, "It would be best for you to see how things stand there. Go ahead and make your presence known to the judge. And *don't* make any waves. Got it?"

"Yes."

"Okay. Call me on my cell phone once you know the details. You'll probably have news before I will."

"All right, I'll talk to you tomorrow. Thanks, Matt."

Taking a deep breath, she ended the call. As she leaned forward to drop the phone into her bag again, car headlights pierced the semidarkness of the living room.

Sam Robertson had come home.

With suddenly unsteady hands, Kayla tugged at her shirt and brushed her hair into place. As battle preparation, it wasn't much, but she had to do what she could to get ready.

Because she *was* going to wage a war against the man.

To this day, the stories Ronnie had told her about him had the power to make Kayla shudder. Stories of his angry silences and then his verbal abuse and, finally, much worse… Kayla had seen proof of it herself, when she'd come to help Ronnie pack up and leave.

Now, she *had* to find a way to take Becky home where she belonged—where she would be safe from this man—even if it meant fighting Sam and the judge and anyone else who tried to get between her and her niece.

Footsteps sounded on the front porch. She braced herself for Sam's entrance.

The door latch rattled and, after a pause, a key scraped in the lock. The door swung open.

Sam stood haloed by the overhead fixture. The harsh lighting washed out his skin and left his face and eyes haggard.

Then he stepped back to help his mother maneuver through the doorway. She moved slowly, on crutches.

Kayla hurried across the room. "Can I—?"

"I've got it."

At his curt tone, she stopped short.

His mother looked at her through eyes heavy-lidded with pain.

Sam merely glared. After a quick glance at Becky, still lying sprawled in sleep, he turned his attention to his mother. "Do you want one of the couches tonight?"

"No," she said, her voice faint. "My bedroom." When Sam reached for her, she attempted a halfhearted protest.

"You're in no shape to manage those stairs by yourself."

Kayla could see the truth of that. She stepped back and returned to the couch. Hands clenched on her knees, she waited while Sam carried his mother to her room.

A while later, she heard him on the stairs again, his boots loud on the uncarpeted wood. He entered the living room and halted several feet away from her.

The only light came from the overhead she had left on in the kitchen.

He looked at her, gave a curt nod. "You got my message?"

"Yes, from Jack." The ranch manager had stopped in several times earlier and at one point had relayed the news. "He told me the emergency room had a crowd. I hope your mother didn't have to wait long in pain." When he said nothing, she added, "And I can see they've given her something to help her sleep."

"Yeah." He glanced at the mantel clock. "It's late. You'll stay the night. You can head out first thing tomorrow."

A statement, not a question. And very grudgingly offered. It didn't matter. She wasn't leaving the next morning, no matter what he wanted. He definitely wouldn't like it when he found out what she had planned.

Much as she hated the idea of his mother's suffering, she knew the disruption to Sam's home life had played right into her hands. Any judge would have to see that.

Sam looked over at Becky.

Even in the low lighting, Kayla could tell the rugged lines of his face never changed. Suddenly, she no longer cared what he thought. Still, it took a surprising amount of effort to drag her gaze away. Weariness, that's all. Lack of sleep had slowed her reactions, made her feel slightly dazed.

"Couldn't get her to bed?" he asked.

"No." She forced a civilized tone. "She was overstimulated after watching you leave in such a hurry. And then from learning about your mother."

"You told her?"

"Only that her grandma wasn't feeling well and you'd taken her to see a doctor."

He nodded.

Becky had nearly bounced off the couch in her excitement at having Kayla there, too. But he wouldn't want to know about that.

"By the time I could get her settled down to eat, she'd gotten overtired." Kayla had found enough food in the refrigerator to make a light dinner for them both. Afterward, she played with her niece until the time came for her to change into pajamas and brush her teeth. But when Kayla put both hands together near her cheek, making the sign for *bed,* Becky unexpectedly balked. "I decided to let her curl up here with her dolls, figuring a few hours on the couch wouldn't hurt. Eventually, she dropped off to sleep."

She'd told herself she didn't want Becky upstairs in an unfamiliar house, anyway. The truth was, she couldn't bear to have her niece separated from her again so soon.

"Well," Sam said, "let's get her up there now. I'll show you where you can bed down for the night." He lifted the sleeping child from the couch and cradled her against him.

This time, as he looked down at her, his expression softened. His eyes gleamed. Silver-gray in the soft lighting and so much like Becky's, those eyes clearly revealed his thoughts. They showed feelings Kayla didn't want to see and emotions she didn't want to believe a man like Sam could have.

Her throat tightened.

He turned slowly away.

Blinking hard, she grabbed the two dolls from the couch and followed him, giving herself a stern lecture. A man who had ignored his daughter for her entire life, who had treated his wife the way he had done, didn't deserve Kayla's sympathy. Or her respect. Or anything else.

She stopped by the front door only long enough to grab the overnight bag she'd taken out of the trunk of the rental car earlier that evening. Another bone of contention. She clenched her jaw in annoyance, thinking again of how he'd trapped her on his ranch.

He turned on the light at the top of the stairs. She forced her jaw to relax and quietly followed him to the second floor. Now wasn't the time to call him on his trick.

She skimmed her free hand along the oak railing, which ended in an intricately carved newel post at the head of a broad, open hall.

They passed a closed door. His mother's room, Kayla assumed, as all the other doors stood open.

Stopping at the next room, he eased sideways, careful of Becky's head and feet as he carried her inside. The matching youth bed and scaled-down dresser proclaimed this a child's room.

She hurried forward to turn down the comforter so Sam could set Becky on the bed. As she looked at her niece, she felt determination fill her again. That little girl had stolen her heart the first minute she'd seen her. Kayla would do whatever it took to make sure Becky had what she needed—including pressing her advantage in this unexpected situation.

She swallowed hard, trying to dislodge the lump that had formed in her throat. Eager for any distraction, she ran her fingertips along the headboard of the bed. Across the width of it had been carved an intricate design of a horse in full gallop, his mane streaming out behind him. "Beautiful," she said sincerely. "I've never seen a design like this before."

"Thanks." The word came grudgingly.

Kayla finished tucking her niece in, placing the two dolls on the pillows on either side of her. "Amazing that she slept through being carried up here," she murmured.

"Worn-out from playing."

She shook her head. "Completely exhausted," she corrected. "She must be. Becky's sensitive to movement and normally wakes up at a touch."

From the other side of the bed, Sam turned as if to leave.

Quickly, she glanced around the room. "There's no night-light in here."

He shrugged.

She looked at him pointedly. "Most small children don't like to sleep in total darkness. For Becky especially, in a strange house, it would help for her to have some extra light."

He nodded but kept going, murmuring over his shoulder, "We left the hall fixture on last night."

That was something, anyhow. Probably his mother's idea.

She followed him out of the room.

On the other side of the hallway, he went ahead of her into a spacious bedroom. On the wall opposite them was a deep bay window. To their left, sliding doors indicated a wall-to-wall closet.

"All yours. *For the night.*" After gesturing at the bed, he walked away, evidently not planning to say another word. He had gone through the doorway before she could think.

"Excuse me," she said.

He turned back.

She took a deep breath. Everything hinged on how she worded what she needed to say. On how well she could convince this man of her sincerity without letting him guess her ulterior motive. "I know you're planning to go to court tomorrow. I don't think you'll get anywhere. You've never had custody of Becky before. You've never even seen her until yesterday."

"And whose fault is that?"

She couldn't get into all that now. She wanted to convince him, not provoke him.

"Now your mother's incapacitated, for who knows how long. How can you possibly take care of Becky?"

The look on his face told her he couldn't. But he rallied, saying bluntly, "I'll find a nanny agency."

"What good will that do? She needs someone with more training than your usual babysitter or nanny. Someone who can talk with her in a language she can understand." The stiffness of his posture said he knew this already. She pressed home her advantage. "What are the chances the agency can fill those requirements?"

"I'll worry about that when I see the applicants."

She struggled to keep her voice level. "We talked about this earlier—I asked if Becky could understand you. Do you know any ASL at all?"

Of course he didn't. She'd bet her last school paycheck for the summer on it.

Reluctantly, she considered his defense. Sam Robertson had never seen his daughter, but that shouldn't matter. He could have—should have—learned to sign so he would be ready to talk to her when they met. *If* they ever met—

She stopped in midthought. Where was she going with this mental argument with herself? Of course, she knew how important it was for people to be able to communicate with Becky. But she also knew what Sam was like.

Now, he stood squinting at her, as if trying to focus across a great distance. That and the sudden chill in his expression startled her. She wasn't sure if he'd even heard her. After a moment, she squared her shoulders and changed her tactic.

"Obviously you don't know ASL." He looked blank. "American Sign Language. You don't know how to sign, do you?"

"Well, no, but—"

"Her grandmother doesn't know how to talk to Becky, either, does she?" Kayla asked.

No squinting from him now, just a hard, cold-eyed look as he stared her down. A muscle in his cheek flexed. "The two of them manage just fine."

The two of them. No mention of himself at all. Or of his mother knowing ASL. Everything she'd seen and heard only reinforced what Ronnie had told the family about him.

Sam Robertson was uncaring to the bone, except when it came to money and working day and night on this ranch.

And it only confirmed what Kayla had feared. Becky had no one here who could communicate with her, no one who truly loved her.

She tried to soften her tone. But she couldn't.

"Your mother's not able to take care of Becky," she continued, "and won't be for the foreseeable future. You can't get a qualified caretaker. What are you going to do with Becky in the unlikely event a judge sides in your favor? Keep her stranded out on this ranch with no one who can talk to her?"

He said nothing, and she barely stopped herself from thumping her fist to her forehead, little finger held upright in the sign for *idiot*.

Panic pushed her on. "You don't even know her," she said, her voice breaking.

Again, he stayed silent.

He wasn't going to let her walk out of here with Becky. She could see that now. It had been foolish even to think she had a chance.

That didn't mean she had given up or even given way.

Her determination was as strong as ever. Becky deserved that. Becky deserved everything any other child had.

Father or no, Sam had never been a parent to her niece. So Kayla would do whatever needed to be done.

She moved to stand directly in front of him, forcing him to look at her. To listen. Just as she would when Becky—in one of her infrequent stubborn moods—refused to give Kayla her full attention.

She would offer him one last opportunity to do the right thing.

"You've got a problem," she said flatly. "But we've got the perfect solution right here. I can communicate with Becky. And she's known me as far back as she can remember. Let me take her home with me."

He narrowed his eyes, now gleaming in the light. "No way in hell."

She swallowed her instinctive response.

"Fine," she said in a clipped voice, blinking back angry tears, hanging on to control as firmly as she could manage. She couldn't worry any longer about trying to convince him of anything. Only Becky mattered. "I'll be going along with you to court tomorrow morning. We'll see what the judge has to say about a man who wants to condemn his four-year-old daughter to solitude."

Barely registering Sam's shocked expression, she stepped back and slammed the bedroom door in his face.

Chapter Three

Unbelievable.

Kayla took a second glance around the town square of Flagman's Folly, which looked like the backdrop of every cowboy movie she'd ever seen. A row of hitching posts circled the perimeter of the square. Well-used horse troughs lined each of the pathways leading to the buildings in the center of the grass-filled area. Instead of water, the troughs now overflowed with some kind of prickly-looking cactus. Pretty, though, with their bright yellow blooms.

She shot a sideways glance at Sam, who looked very prickly himself. Earlier that morning, at the ranch, he had thrown out every argument he could, but Kayla stood her ground.

She would appear with him in court, and that was that.

Holding tightly to Becky's hand, she followed Sam up the steps and through the wide double doorway of the Town Hall. Their footsteps echoed loudly on the wooden floor as they walked across the entryway.

In the courtroom, the judge ruled from behind a massive wooden bench set beneath a revolving white ceiling fan.

One look at the Honorable Lloyd M. Baylor, and

Kayla felt her confidence wilt. She was no tough, thorny desert cactus.

More like a water-starved bouquet.

The man could easily pass for a throwback to a Western movie judge himself, with his hair styled into a thinning white pompadour. An aging Elvis impersonator, minus the sideburns. Through the unfastened neck of his black robe, she could see a shirt collar held together by a string tie ending in hammered silver tips. When he prepared to leave the courtroom, it wouldn't surprise her a bit to see him buckle on a low-slung belt carrying a couple of six-shooters. Meanwhile, behind the desk, he wielded his gavel like a weapon.

Even as Kayla settled Becky in the first row of spectators' benches, her hands began to tremble. What were the chances a good old boy like that would favor her over the outstanding citizen standing before him?

Sure enough, from the lofty height of his bench, the judge's bright blue eyes lasered in on Sam, giving preference to the local over the outsider. "And what brings you to my courtroom on this fine morning, young Robertson?" he asked in a slow, Southern drawl.

Worse, his words held a familiarity that made Kayla stiffen with dread. After quickly signing *Okay?* to Becky, who nodded her response, Kayla hurried to Sam's side.

"Now, Judge." The court clerk, a wiry older woman with faded brown hair and lively eyes, stood near his elbow. She leaned even closer and said, "You know just what this is all about. And you'll want to get a move on with it, else you'll be late for dinner."

He raised his brows and made a show of pulling back the robe's sleeve to look at his watch. "Ellamae, it's nine-fifteen in the a.m."

She beamed. "My point exactly."

"Hmm. Well, let's get this show going, then. But, first, we'll mind our manners." The judge turned in Kayla's direction. "Morning, young lady. And exactly who might you be?"

She took a deep breath and plunged in. "I'm Kayla Ward, Becky's aunt." She pointed to Becky, who sat playing with her doll. "I've come here to take her home with me."

"You can't," Sam said. "She's mine, as of two days ago. And I intend to make the situation permanent. Judge, I want full custody of my daughter."

Kayla gasped. She hadn't expected him to state his case immediately. "*No!* That's not right. He hadn't even seen Becky until—"

"Yeah?" Sam countered. "You can just thank your sister—"

The judge banged his gavel and the noise startled them both into silence. Kayla dropped her hands to her sides.

Judge Baylor had slammed his gavel firmly enough to cause Becky to look across the room. He waggled his fingers at her and smiled, as if he'd only wanted her attention so he could say hello. She grinned, waved and returned to playing with her doll.

The judge sat back and focused on Sam again. "Young man, this is a court of law," he intoned. "You'll keep a civil tongue here, unless you want me to hold you in contempt."

Kayla fought a sigh of relief. Maybe her chances weren't as hopeless as she'd thought. "One for my side," she murmured.

"Sorry, Judge." Sam's tone sounded contrite, but she

couldn't find a bit of remorse in the steely gray gaze he shot her way.

"And you, young lady." She snapped her head up to meet a second pair of unyielding eyes. "My hearing's good as it ever was. If you don't mind, I'll be the one keeping score in this courtroom."

"Yes, sir."

"'Your Honor' will do me fine." He looked briefly toward the spectators' benches before turning to Kayla. "You're countering this man's request. On what grounds?"

She swallowed hard, then said in a rush, "I want full custody, Your Honor. On the grounds that Mr. Robertson is not fit to take care of Becky."

"You *what?*" Sam loomed closer. "And the hell I'm not—"

"According to Ronnie—"

"Who couldn't tell the truth if she—"

Bang!

"Second warning." The judge glared at them both. "And as Ellamae here can attest, you won't want to pay the penalty that comes of making it to number three. I'm surprised at you, Sam Robertson. With all your shenanigans, you, at least, ought to know how I run my courtroom."

Shenanigans? What could that mean? Sam had a history of trouble? Possibly even a court record? Kayla made a mental note to find out more about this. To find anything that would give her some leverage without having to make Ronnie's story public.

The judge set the gavel down on the bench. "Now, it's my understanding you're here fighting for the responsibility to care for that child sitting in the first pew. Let's get at this another way." He looked at Sam. "Your request for custody's come up fairly suddenly. The ink's barely dry on Ellamae's paperwork. Now, exactly how did all this come about?"

Sam explained the details of Ronnie's appearance at the ranch with Becky and Sharleen's story of the conversation.

The judge frowned. "I can't take steps on something this serious just on your mama's word. *Or* on that other woman's say-so. These things have to be handled properly. Legally."

"But, Judge, her mother agreed to turn responsibility for her over to me."

"And my responsibility is to the court—and, by extension, that little girl. Now, you're telling me that ex of yours is giving up the child, after so many years?" The judge frowned. "Unusual, isn't it?"

"I don't know."

"Then I'll tell you. It's downright unusual." He swung his gaze back to Kayla. "And it's even more peculiar, at least in my courtroom, to have someone besides a parent put a foot into proceedings like this one. You, ma'am, feel the need to contest the mama's wishes? *And* the daddy's?"

"Yes, Your Honor," Kayla said, an uncalculated tremor in her voice, "I do. I've helped raise Becky since the day she was born. I love her, and I want her with me."

She could hear Sam's exhalation. The back of her neck prickled as if his breath had touched her. Trying to block out all thoughts of him, she took a half step forward. She needed to focus on the one person in the room who could give her what she wanted.

"Your Honor," she continued earnestly, "my niece is deaf. Becky needs someone to watch over her who can communicate with her, something Sam—Mr. Robertson—isn't capable of doing."

Sam closed in on her again, clenching his hands into fists. She wouldn't have much more time to state her case before he exploded into speech.

"I'm a teacher, Your Honor. What's more, I teach American Sign Language, the *only* language Becky knows. I have a deaf sister and learned to sign with her long before Becky was born. I can talk with her. Sam can't. Besides," she rushed on, "he doesn't have a relationship with her. He's never had one. They're strangers to each other. Becky doesn't know him at all."

Judge Baylor stared at her for a moment, then gave an understanding nod and glanced over toward Becky. Kayla's heart suddenly felt lighter. She didn't dare look sideways.

Finally, turning back to her, the judge said, "The child and her daddy haven't seen each other in years, and now you want to take her away?"

"I—" Kayla's throat tightened at his unexpectedly accusing words and tone. She had to swallow hard before she could speak. "Your Honor, she's been with me, with my family, since birth."

"True enough." He nodded. "And it seems to me only fair for her daddy to take his turn. Now's the perfect time for him to get to know his little girl."

"But, Your Honor—"

"Sounds great—"

This time, Judge Baylor simply lifted a finger, forcing them both into silence. He stared down at his hands, now folded on the desk in front of him.

The only sound came from the whirring of the fan above them, a rhythmic swishing noise that seemed to echo the pulse beating in Kayla's ears. The judge wouldn't make Becky stay with Sam. He couldn't.

At last, he spoke. "Let's not rush into things here. The child herself needs some exposure to her daddy's life, something she's never had a chance to experience. She can meet some of the folks out in the community, too." He smiled. "We've got us a nice little town here, if I do say so myself. And I know everyone will welcome that little girl with open arms. After all, she's part of the history of Flagman's Folly."

"Your Honor, please," Kayla burst out. "With all due respect, Becky doesn't understand about history." Near the judge's elbow, the court clerk swung her hand across her throat in an emphatic cut-it-off-*now* warning, but Kayla felt too upset to care. "Besides, what is the point of having her get to meet people? I don't intend to stay here with her. She'll go back with me to Chicago. And—"

"Forget that," Sam yelled. "Becky's not going anywhere."

The gavel slammed again. Kayla would have sworn the blades of the overhead fan jumped from the vibration.

The judge slapped his hand on the bench. "We seem to have lost track of the fact that *I'm* the one who makes the decisions around here." Slowly, he shook his head. "Young Robertson, I'm ashamed of you. And you, as well, little lady. That's a child you two are fighting over, not a roping calf you're chasing to see which one of you can bring her home."

Judge Baylor's face had turned red with anger.

Ellamae, the court clerk, gave a resigned shrug and stared at the floor.

Kayla looked away, blinking hard against a sudden rush of tears.

Beside her, Sam shifted uneasily.

The judge was right. But how could she *not* fight for Becky? How could she not look out for her niece's welfare, something Becky's own father had never done?

"As I see it," Judge Baylor began again, "for all intents and purposes, Becky's mama abandoned her little girl, and here you both are wanting to tear the child apart in my courtroom. I won't have it." He glared. "I won't even entertain a thought about that child's future until her present life has had a chance to settle. That's not a matter for negotiation." He rapped the gavel again. Then he stood, bracing his hand on the bench, looming over them.

Kayla stiffened to attention. From the corner of her eye, she could see Sam doing the same.

"Let me just add," the judge said, his voice ringing through the courtroom, "that I will look unfavorably upon noncooperation. From either party." He stared them down in turn.

Kayla wiped her suddenly damp palms against her pant legs, then grasped the fabric and held on tight. She fought to hold her tongue, too. The man might be only a caricature compared to the several judges she'd met socially in Chicago, but he wielded the power in this courtroom. She couldn't afford to get on his bad side.

If she hadn't already.

"Now." He sank back into his leather swivel chair. "Obviously, at the present moment, we're not within spitting distance of a nice, happy resolution. Neither of you will walk out of here today with the outcome you desire." He cleared his throat and glanced toward Becky. "But we do have the child to consider. In my estimation, there's only one reasonable and beneficent thing I can do in her regard." He stared at Kayla and Sam again. "And we *do* want reasonable and beneficent where that child is concerned, do we not?"

They all nodded, including Ellamae.

"All right, then. I'm going to table both requests for full custody. *For the moment.* Until we track down the mama and look into the matter further."

"I have someone trying to locate her," Kayla said eagerly.

"Very helpful, I'm sure," the judge drawled, raising his brows. "And young lady, you said you're a teacher?"

"Yes, Your Honor," she replied, her heart soaring.

"And you teach sign language up there in Chicago?"

"Yes! Yes, I do." She clasped her trembling hands in front of her.

He beamed. "Well then, I ask you, what could be more perfect? You're off for a bit now, isn't that right?"

"Yes, I am. And it *is* a perfect time, Your Honor. I would have all summer with Becky in Chicago. All the time in the world to be with her and—"

Smiling, the judge raised his hand. "Not exactly what I'm setting forth this morning. Sam, the child's here now, in your home. Let's give it some time for the two of you to get acquainted. Six weeks, shall we say?"

Kayla nearly choked holding back her protest. The judge turned to her.

"Young lady, you've got all that time, you can stay here for the summer. Help take care of the child. And help her learn to get along with her daddy." He looked from Kayla to Sam and back again. "The pair of you can make a genuine effort to show her the two most important adults in her life are in agreement. And while you're at it, you might have a thought or two about finding some common ground." He tapped his gavel on the desk. "I'll award you both temporary joint custody—"

"Judge—"

"Your Honor—"

"Shh!" Eyes wide, Ellamae slapped a finger against her lips. The gesture meant the same thing in *both* languages spoken in the room.

"—unless," Judge Baylor continued as if there had been no interruption, "I deem it necessary to make other arrangements." He spoke slowly, giving ominous weight to his every word. "According to Sam, here, the mama's ready to give up her parental rights. Seeing as that's the case, it would not be outside the bounds of this court to place the child in a foster home until the matter is resolved."

Kayla swallowed her moan. Beside her, Sam covered his harsh indrawn breath with a cough.

"At this very moment," the judge went on, adding even more of a twang to his drawl, "I'm not inclined to do that. This bonding of the child with her daddy, getting to know each other..." He circled his hand in the air. "These things will take time. In the meanwhile, I feel it is in the best interests of the child to be in the care of both parties concerned." His hand stopped in midair. His white eyebrows shot up and stayed in place. "Are we in agreement here?"

"Yes, sir," Sam spoke up.

"Yes, Your Honor," Kayla added hastily.

"Good. That's settled. Ellamae, you put a notice on the calendar for another six weeks. And Sam, you give Sharleen my best regards. Let her know I'm looking forward to a barbecue out at your place one Sunday soon."

Sam nodded.

Judge Baylor rose.

Becky looked over at them, and he smiled and waved.

"Young lady," he said to Kayla, "ask that little one if she knows who this man is." He gestured to Sam.

Unwillingly, Kayla complied with the judge's request. Using her right hand, she pointed to Sam, then touched her crooked thumb and index finger to her chin. With her left hand tucked out of sight against her side, she crossed her fingers so tightly, her arm shook. *Please, please, don't let Becky know.* The child's confusion would confirm what Kayla had tried to prove all along.

Her niece grinned, raised her open hand in the air and tapped her thumb on her forehead.

Her heart breaking, Kayla dutifully voiced what Becky had signed. "She said *Daddy.*"

"SAM. MISS WARD."

Sam stopped and turned. He should've known he wouldn't get away without a dressing-down from Ellamae.

Beside him, Kayla signed to Becky, who nodded and climbed onto a seat in the last row of benches. She swung her sneakered feet back and forth, the toes of the shoes almost touching the floor tiles.

Sam's throat tightened. Already so grown-up, and he'd never even had the chance to see her as a baby.

Ellamae stopped in front of them, then peered over her shoulder at the door Judge Baylor had closed firmly in his wake. Turning back, she stared at Sam for a long minute. Ellamae had known him since birth and never hesitated to speak her mind. He braced himself. But to his surprise, she directed her words to Kayla.

"You best heed what the judge told you about little Becky. He'll expect your cooperation."

"That's pointless—"

Ellamae raised her hand, halting Kayla in midsentence. "No sense mouthing off to me about it, missy. You heard the judge."

"This is so ridiculous."

"This is a small town," Ellamae corrected mildly.

Sam couldn't argue with her there. To tell the truth, he didn't mind seeing the older woman taking Kayla Ward down a few pegs.

"You best heed *that,* too," Ellamae added, "and watch how you handle yourself with the townsfolk."

Kayla frowned, and Sam just knew a sarcastic response hovered on her lips. Fortunately for her—because she definitely didn't want to go locking horns with Ellamae—a vibrating noise came from the bag slung across Kayla's shoulder. She dug into the bag and pulled out a cell phone. While she didn't actually smile, her face relaxed.

She was a hell of a good-looking woman—when she wasn't glaring at him. For a minute there, as she'd fought with the judge for Becky, he'd forgotten himself and stared at her in admiration. She had more spunk and spark than Ronnie had ever had—cool, beautiful Ronnie who'd turned into the coldest, conniving-est…

Well, she didn't matter. Neither of them did.

After the momentary lapse while looking at Kayla, he came to his senses. This, he reminded himself, was the woman who had flown to his wife's side years ago and had helped take his yet-to-be-born child away from him.

Now she was trying it again.

Seemed every time she showed up, he stood to lose something.

She waved the phone at him. "I've got to answer this message," she said. "I'll go outside with Becky."

Sam took a step forward. Again, he knew what to expect, and there it came, the blue-eyed glare meant to freeze him in place.

"Right outside," she said emphatically, pointing into the hall. A long window seat lined the wall opposite the courtroom.

Reluctantly, he nodded.

She gestured to Becky, and the two of them left the room.

She'd barely taken her seat when Ellamae turned to him. Again, he readied himself for her lecture. He had only a second to wait.

"And you, mister." She poked a bony forefinger into his chest. "You shouldn't need any convincing at all about what I'm trying to say. The judge has got strong opinions about kinfolk and will want that little girl to get to know her daddy. He'll expect you *and* Miss Ward to be out and about with the child."

"That's ridiculous." Like he had the time—and the money—to spend the next six weeks escorting that woman around town. "I don't need to put Becky on parade to get to know her."

"You don't think so?" She sighed in exasperation. "Are you thinking *at all* right now, boy? How do you expect the judge to find out if you're following his order or not? My suggestion—take the child to town as much as you can. That's the only way word will get back to him."

"I'm not—"

"Sam!" Her voice rose. "I'm telling you, with your

history, the judge is *not* going to make things easy for you."

Sam glanced quickly into the hallway. Kayla's eyes met his. She didn't look away, waver, or even blink, just stared him down. Only the need to keep his past in the past kept him from snapping back at Ellamae's words.

"That's not all," she continued now.

He noticed with relief that she had lowered her voice, though it still held an urgent tone. "What it boils down to is, he wants that child to get comfortable with you. And you to do likewise with her."

Ellamae narrowed her eyes, but that did nothing to hide the concern in them. As she often reminded him, she and his grandmother had cut their baby teeth together. Ellamae claimed that gave her more right than most people to interfere in his life.

"You come from a long line of pigheaded Robertsons, Sam." Her expression crumpled, along with the pretense of stern reproach. She put her hand on his forearm and shook it. "Don't let that stubborn streak cost you. The judge can be just as obstinate, and he's got a long memory. You know well enough about that."

Sam stiffened. Yes, he knew. He'd made a bad choice way back at age seventeen. A choice that had set him on a wrong road. That had led to a whole list of stupid decisions, including turning wild as a teenager and eventually winding up married to a woman he couldn't trust.

He'd come close to getting thrown in jail, and only Sharleen's pleas and the recent death of his daddy had bought Sam any leniency from the judge at all. And though his mother had forgiven Sam for everything, he had never forgiven himself.

Ellamae edged closer to him and lowered her voice even further. "Between you, me and these four walls, boy, I'll warn you. I've no doubt this child is just as much a surprise to you as she is to the rest of us. But you can't just expect to show up in court six weeks from now and think the judge'll hand over custody to you. He'll have spies *everywhere* in the meantime, reporting back to him on your actions."

"Hasn't he always?" Sam muttered.

She glared. "Look, bad blood between the two of you or not, you have to admit the man's got a heart. Otherwise, you'd have spent time rotting in jail. And he won't tell you this, so I'm saying it to you myself. He's keeping that child's welfare—and *only* that child's welfare—in mind. He's got to hear folks have seen you around town, acting like a real daddy with her." She slapped his forearm. "And don't you dare risk losing your little girl just because you and missy out there in the hallway don't see eye to eye."

Nodding grimly, he looked toward the hall again. Kayla sat holding her phone in front of her, her thumbs tapping rapidly over the keypad.

He stiffened, wondering just what message she was sending. And who she was sending it to.

Ellamae patted his arm and turned away.

Feeling suddenly unsteady, Sam gripped the top of the high wooden bench his daughter had occupied a few minutes ago. Somehow, in just a couple of days, his entire life had gotten thrown into an upheaval. He had to get things settled again.

Ellamae would find a way to spread the news of his child's existence to everyone in the county. He knew it. Folks would get over the shock the minute they met Becky.

That was *his* job.

Ellamae was right. His history in this courtroom

went back far enough to hurt him. Small towns had long memories, and folks around here held competitions to prove how far back they could dredge up old news. Judge Baylor had them all beat, with a memory older than dirt and longer than the Rio Grande.

Sam would do whatever it took to get the judge to rule in his favor. Even though it would mean making one hell of a sacrifice.

He looked at the woman seated outside in the hallway, her head down as she tapped away at her cell phone.

He had her to thank for this whole predicament.

Chapter Four

TEMPORARY JOINT CUSTODY!

Incensed, Kayla keyed the words in all capital letters on her phone. She knew her sister, Lianne, at the other end of the wireless connection, would understand Kayla's emotion.

Lianne knew how close Kayla was to Becky. How much Kayla loved their niece. Lianne loved her, too, though she hadn't spent as much time with her. She didn't feel responsible for Becky.

She didn't feel, as Kayla did, as if she were Becky's second mother.

TEMPORARY JOINT CUSTODY! She read the message again, then continued, This is crazy.

Not crazy, the answer came back. Good for you. You can see her every day.

In Sam Robertson's company.

Compromise. That's life.

Kayla bit back a laugh. My life, maybe. What about his? A pointless question. I never expected him to argue with me over Becky. I planned to just pack up her belongings and come home. Well, if I have to keep fighting, I will.

But she couldn't dispute the judge's order.

And what about Sam's obvious suspicion that she would run off with her niece? He'll never give me time alone with Becky.

Except…

Thumbs over the keypad, she froze. Could what she'd just realized really be true? She thought hard, nodded once and continued keying furiously.

I need to convince Sam to let me live at the ranch.

His mom's laid up, isn't she? Lianne shot back.

Kayla almost laughed aloud. You're one step ahead of me! An excuse to stick close to Becky AND Sam. A chance to find something to sway the judge in my favor.

Again, Lianne caught on. Dig up some dirt on Sam. So the judge will give you Becky.

Yes!

Devious, Lianne responded. I like it.

Me, too.

Staying close to Sam would buy her time, and with luck she'd find evidence to use against him. Her conscience twinged, but she firmly pushed the feeling away.

This was for Becky's sake. She couldn't leave her niece with a man Ronnie said wasn't a fit father.

She didn't know how the child's own mother could have done that, either.

Shaking her head, she texted, Any word from Ronnie?

Not yet.

Maybe Matt had found her already.

But Kayla knew, no matter what she learned from Ronnie, she would have to win this battle on her own.

One after another, ideas clicked into place. She could fight for her niece by working her way into Sam's life. By finding out what she could about him from his mother and the men who worked on his ranch. From his neighbors and friends in town. From the man himself.

She could investigate Sam on a local level. And maybe find out enough to avoid bringing everything about Ronnie's life with him into the open.

She thumbed the keypad again swiftly. Already talked to Matt Lawrence. He's trying to locate Ronnie.

Good. Now—what to tell Mom and Dad?

Kayla pressed her lips together and hit the keypad without hesitation. Will be back soon—with Becky.

Sounds great. Need me? Lianne asked.

Always. Just texting the word brought a lump to Kayla's throat.

They had spent so many of their childhood years apart when their parents sent Lianne to a school for deaf children. Kayla had been heartbroken by the separation and feared she and Lianne would never have an "always" together. When Lianne had returned home for her high school years, Kayla had been elated—and proud to introduce all her friends to the sister she looked up to.

Kayla shook off the memories.

I can handle it here, she continued. I could use some clothes, etc., though. Will email you a list. Can you overnight a box to me?

Sure. On standby. Good luck.

Sam exited the courtroom and stopped in front of her. A scowl darkened his features, and he gave an impatient look toward the outside door.

Kayla knew she would need all the luck she could get, starting now.

She texted a quick goodbye and stowed the phone in her bag. Then, hastily, she rose to face Sam, hoping at least to put them in equal power positions.

Unfortunately, she couldn't measure up. He stood a head taller and his shoulders seemed a mile wider.

Before either one of them could speak, another man walked down the hall. As he moved to pass them, Sam stepped forward to give him more room. The man continued on his way.

Sam stayed where he was in front of Kayla. Much too close in the narrow hallway. Much too disturbing to her peace of mind.

Funny. She'd never suffered from claustrophobia before, but all of a sudden she found herself almost choking from a lack of air.

She gripped the strap of her shoulder bag and sucked in a steadying breath. "We need to talk. But there are too many people around here. Can't we find somewhere more private?"

Sam hooted a laugh, throwing his head back and gesturing widely with his arms.

Becky looked up at him.

"Private?" he repeated. "Honey, it's obvious you're a stranger to Flagman's Folly. There's not a place in town where people don't hang around with their ears flapping, trying to catch everything that's going on." He leaned even closer, and the scent of mint-flavored toothpaste reached her.

She shuffled back a step. The window seat caught her behind the knees. She had nowhere else to go. And not a sensible word of reply in her brain. She blurted the only thing she could think of to say. "Don't call me 'honey.'"

"Fine. But I'll call your bluff on that request for a talk." Spiky dark brows, a match to his midnight-black hair, nearly met above his eyes as he glared down at her. "I've got plenty of things to say to you, too. And I guarantee you're not going to like any of them."

KAYLA FUMED SILENTLY in the passenger seat as Sam maneuvered his dust-covered pickup truck away from their parking spot in front of Town Hall.

"I might as well start introducing Becky around town," Sam said, sounding both irritated and determined.

She glanced back at her niece and got a stranglehold on her door handle. If only it were a lever for an ejector seat that could catapult them both to Chicago in the blink of an eye.

She had thought—*hoped*—that Sam would refuse to follow orders and that *she* could set the good example and win points with the judge.

"It ought to be fairly quiet at the Double S," he continued. "And it's right down the street. We can talk there and have a drink while we're at it."

"A *drink?*" Her jaw dropped.

He looked at her fleetingly, then back to the road in front of him. His mouth curled in a sarcastic smile.

"What are you *thinking?*" she asked, unable to hold back her outrage. "You can't take a child into a bar. They must have laws against that, even out here in the wild, wild West. Just as they have laws for child seats in moving vehicles."

Fortunately, Kayla had come prepared—for what she had thought would be her quick return to Chicago. Now she looked pointedly over her shoulder at the booster chair she had strapped into the backseat. Becky held her doll close to the half window, allowing her to see the sights, too.

Not that there were a lot to be found on this tiny stretch of so-called civilization in the middle of nowhere. And, other than the grass around Town Hall and the cactus plants in the water troughs, she hadn't seen much of anything green. Of course, in all honesty, there wasn't much vegetation in her urban neighborhood back home, either.

Still wearing that mocking smile, Sam looked over at her again. "You must not get out much, if you think this is the wild West. Anyhow, the Double S isn't a bar. It's a café. With great coffee."

"Oh." Well, she'd already made her point over the safety seat. "I don't drink coffee."

"It figures."

Less than the length of a city block away from Town Hall, he parked the truck in front of a squat, stuccoed building. Kayla rushed to unbuckle her seat belt, then to free Becky from hers.

After helping her niece jump from the truck's high cab, Kayla glanced at the café.

A clever hand-painted sign above the front door showed one *S* swinging playfully from a second one. A trellised archway of amazingly lifelike flowers and curling vines, also hand-painted, wound around the entry. Terra-cotta pots filled with flowering cacti lined the walls on either side of the door. A pair of wooden shutters framed each window. The restaurant's outward appearance was clean, quaint and well cared for.

She was curious to see if that impression held inside the café.

Becky looked from the building to Sam and Kayla, then brushed her open hand in the air in front of her face and pulled her fingertips together.

"Pretty," Kayla voiced for Sam's benefit. She bobbed her fist in the air and repeated the sign. *"Yes, it's pretty."*

Inside, the Southwestern theme continued with unvarnished wooden tables and chairs and rough woven place mats. The only jarring note came from a thoroughly modern glass display case at one end of the counter in the rear of the café, its shelves filled with cakes and cookies and pastries. Becky noticed the goodies, too, and headed right toward them. Kayla smiled.

After a glance at Sam, she stopped smiling.

Early that morning, he had said his mother planned to spend the day in her room. Kayla prepared a meal for him to carry upstairs. Before leaving the kitchen, he abruptly announced he'd already eaten breakfast. Then he walked out, returning only in time to leave for town.

Kayla had shrugged. To tell the truth, she'd been dreading the first meal with all of them together. Still, she couldn't help a feeling of irritation on Becky's behalf. Just when did Sam Robertson intend to begin getting acquainted with his own daughter?

Now Kayla shrugged again, no longer bothered by his actions. It would be much better for *her* plans if Sam didn't get close to Becky at all. If only he hadn't come up with the idea to stop by this café, either.

She turned to look at her niece, who stood staring into the dessert case. She had eaten a good-size serving of eggs and toast that morning, but she had a sweet tooth to rival Kayla's own.

Kayla felt tempted to head toward the dessert case, too.

Instead, she followed Sam to the counter.

As they approached, a petite raven-haired woman in a bright orange waitress's uniform shifted her gaze from Becky to them. She looked about Kayla's mother's age, but the broad smile that lit her face erased years from it.

"Sam, my friend!" she called. She chuckled and indicated the little girl with her hands and nose pressed against the display case. "And this I think must be Becky."

Kayla blinked. Sam hadn't been kidding about people keeping their ears open in this town.

"Yep." He slid onto a stool. When the other woman looked curiously over his shoulder at Kayla, he made brief introductions. "This is Dorinda Martinez. Kayla Ward."

"Nice to meet you, Dorinda."

"The same for me. Call me Dori, please."

"Dori," she agreed, smiling as she took the seat beside Sam.

Did he plan to have their talk in front of this nice but clearly observant woman? Kayla wondered about the "plenty of things" he had to say. Well, she'd just have to take her turn in the conversation first.

"So you've heard about Becky already?" he asked Dori.

"Of course. How was your meeting with the judge this morning?"

At her question, even he did a double take. "How the heck did you find out about that?"

She grinned. "Every day, Ellamae has an order to go on her way to Town Hall."

"Huh. I should've known."

"Two nurses from the hospital came in for coffee and told me about your poor mama, too."

"Hmm. Well, the judge was about what you'd expect," Sam muttered. "Crotchety. Mom's doing fine this morning. Still in some pain. They say a bad sprain's worse than a fracture. But mostly she's just uncomfortable. And—" he gave a low chuckle "—she's no end ticked off that the doc's forcing her to bed rest."

"Sharleen is not one to sit still, is she?"

Kayla fought to keep from frowning. On the way to town, when she had asked Sam about his mother, he'd said merely, "She's okay." He certainly seemed willing enough to talk now.

Dori took a step into the café's kitchen area behind her. "Manny, come see who's here."

A moment later, a dark-haired man appeared, his round face splitting into a grin when he saw Sam. "Hey, my friend. It's been a while."

Now, that didn't surprise Kayla at all. Ronnie had told them how little Sam left the ranch.

"About time you decided to visit," the other man continued. "And *good* timing. I have a pot of five-alarm chili on the back burner, waiting just for you."

Sam shook his head. "A little early for me, thanks, Manny. But the ladies here might want some of Dori's desserts."

"Of course!" Dori said, winking at Kayla. "If not for my sweets, no one would even stop by the café."

"Ha." Manny tilted his head toward Sam. "Coffee?"

He nodded.

"It's true," Dori told Kayla as she moved over to the display case. "People from all over the county come here—"

"For my chili," Manny broke in.

"Ahh, my poor mixed-up husband, we'll let Kayla be the judge of what's good. And Becky." She knelt down beside the little girl and pointed at the display case.

Becky nodded eagerly and put her hand on the glass near a doughnut decorated with chocolate sprinkles.

"One doughnut, coming up," Dori said.

Her throat tight, Kayla nearly croaked out her order to Manny for tea and an apple tart.

It was so easy to communicate with a four-year-old. Yet, all morning, Sam hadn't said a word or even made a gesture toward the child.

How could the judge possibly think about leaving Becky in the care of a man as unfeeling as this? Why didn't Sam try to talk with his own daughter? Even more puzzling, why was he fighting for custody when he obviously didn't want anything to do with Becky?

Desperately needing a distraction from these thoughts,

Kayla said, "Dori and Manny. So, where does the name Double S come in?"

Manny pretended to shudder. "My Dori wanted to call the place Spicy and Sweet. Can you believe?"

"*Sweet* 'n' Spicy," Dori corrected.

He rolled his eyes. "So now it's the Double S."

"Sure. Thanks to my friend here."

"Wait a minute," Sam protested. "It wasn't my idea."

"Oh? Do you think I'll fall for that?" Dori's voice sounded stern, but as she turned toward Kayla, the twinkle in her eyes gave her away. "A cowboy gives my café a cowboy name. And a cowboy makes the sign outside. That's proof, isn't it?"

"Sounds like it to me," Kayla agreed, struggling to hide her shock. *Sam* had made that beautiful, creative sign she had seen at the front of the café? The idea astounded her. When she glanced sideways at him, he looked away.

She thought of the intricately carved headboard on Becky's bed. Had Sam made that, too? The idea made her distinctly uneasy. Had he taken the time, gone to the effort in the hope his daughter might sleep in that bed someday?

How wonderful if Becky's father had thought so much of her.

And how awful for Kayla if the judge found out.

That is, *if* her thoughts were even true. Sam certainly hadn't done anything to support them so far.

She forced her attention back to the conversation.

"Now we are the Double S," Manny was saying. "Short and to the point."

Dori spread her hands wide and shrugged. "It's not polite to refuse a gift. And so I am defeated."

"Keeping our guests from their refreshments isn't polite, either." Manny turned back to them, a brimming teacup in one hand.

"We'll take our stuff over to a table," Sam told him.

"Good enough."

Sam now stood beside his counter stool, waiting.

Kayla slid from her seat.

The time had come for the talk she had requested. If Sam didn't mind having that conversation with his friends in hearing range, she wouldn't let it bother her, either.

She gripped the strap of her shoulder bag and sailed past him.

Chapter Five

Sam pushed his coffee mug from side to side. Dori had Becky occupied at the counter with crayons and paper. Just as he'd settled at the corner table, a steady stream of customers had come in for their midmorning coffee. The place had gotten more crowded than he'd expected. By the time he greeted all the new arrivals and made introductions, he'd begun to think he and Kayla would never get down to business.

Maybe a straight talk at the Double S wasn't such a good idea, but he hated the thought of bringing this woman back to his ranch.

When they were finally as isolated as they would probably get, she beat him to the punch.

"Sam, as I said to you last night, your mother can't get around. She's not going to be able to do much housework or cooking. Or probably even to handle the stairs alone at first." She lifted her hand for a second, then put it flat on the tabletop, almost as if she'd planned to reach out to him. "I'd like to stay at your house and help out."

"Hell, no." A muscle in his cheek flexed.

"Okay." She set her teacup and saucer down in the exact middle of her place mat. "That's fine."

He looked at her warily, knowing she'd never let it rest at that. And she didn't.

"As we were driving here, I noticed there's a bed-and-breakfast nearby. Let me stay there with Becky."

"Yeah, right. I'm supposed to trust you not to take off with her?"

"Of course you can trust me. And the judge *did* give us joint custody. I have every right to be with her when-ever I want. Why would I try to take her away?"

"Why wouldn't you?" he countered. "What's to stop you? You've got a rental car sitting right there at the house."

She looked at him. All the way through him, prob-ably. "Yes. And that's where it will stay when I'm at the ranch. Without having it penned in by other vehicles, if you don't mind."

So she'd seen what Jack had done to her little blue sedan. Looked like she'd gotten the message. *Good.*

"If Becky and your mother and I are alone all day," she continued, "I would need the car in case of emer-gency."

That kept him quiet. After what had just happened to Sharleen, he surely couldn't argue with a need to be prepared.

"Sam, I'm a teacher. I've been fingerprinted for my job and have a clean record. What's more, I'm honest and trustworthy, and you won't have to worry about having me in your home."

"That's not a worry to me at all." He couldn't have made his tone any colder.

"Because you don't plan to let me stay." Her eyes brightened. He stirred restlessly in his seat. "Becky has been 'dumped here,' as you put it, literally with strangers. You've got a ranch to take care of. And you *know* a nanny from some agency won't be able to sign—or worse—to communicate with Becky in an emergency."

Sam forced himself to stare without blinking, without relaxing one bit. He would not let her get to him.

Becky came running over, waving her piece of paper. She slapped it on the table in front of Kayla and snapped her fingers.

From upside down, he saw a brown blob with a couple of floppy additions to it. As little as he could tell about it, the blob could have been anything from a rabbit to a tractor.

"A dog," Kayla said. She looked at the picture, smiled, then brushed one palm briskly across the other. *"Very nice."*

She rose. "I'm going up to get Becky's milk."

The child went along with her, gesturing wildly as they went to the counter. Kayla looked on, signing back to her.

What they were talking about, he hadn't a clue. He never would. Busy as the ranch kept him, what chance in the world would he have of learning another language? Zero to none. Besides, at his age, he probably couldn't pick up on it, anyhow.

He looked at the drawing on the table again. Beside the brown blob Becky had added a green blob that might have been a doghouse. Or an alien.

Damn.

How could he hope to raise his child? He couldn't even understand the kid's drawings!

For a moment, his determination wavered. With both hands, he got a firm grip on his coffee mug as if it could help him hold on to what he really wanted. For Becky to have everything she deserved. Everything she needed.

Was he the one to provide that? Could he care for

her well enough? How could he know? He'd only met the child two days ago. Much too soon to tell.

Did he *want* to take care of her?

Hell, yes.

He couldn't handle this situation as it stood. And he couldn't let that woman up at the counter take advantage of that.

But would he let his pride keep him from doing what he knew was right?

Kayla had spoken the truth. A nanny couldn't take care of Becky in an emergency. She'd hit the nail square-on about Sharleen, too. Much as he didn't want to admit it, he had problems. And only Kayla Ward had answers.

He watched as she talked for a while with Dori before turning to make her way toward their table again. Watched the handful of men in the place look her over, too. Why not? She was a beautiful woman, no doubt about that. And no resemblance to Ronnie at all.

Every time his ex had gone into town, she would dress like she was headed to the city. Big-city prices on those getups, too. Kayla wore more casual clothes, but even in chinos and a silky T-shirt, she seemed as out of place in this town as a heifer in a henhouse. He'd had his fill of beautiful women.

Especially ones named Ward.

She set the half-empty plastic tumbler of milk on the table and took her seat again.

Then she leaned forward. Her lips parted, and for some reason he couldn't help leaning forward a fraction, too.

"I've got the law on my side."

Her words slammed him back against his seat.

She looked steadily at him. "There's no getting

around the fact," she murmured, "that Judge Baylor gave me the right to see my niece—whether you like the idea or not. And I don't want her having to face yet another caretaker right now. You shouldn't, either."

Becky patted Kayla's arm, and she transferred her attention to the child.

Tearing his gaze away, he stared down into his mug again.

She had nerve throwing the decision in his face. As if he could have forgotten the judge's words. But she had a point, too, about the caretaker. He *didn't* want Becky saddled with another babysitter, either. As far as his options went...

Well, he didn't have any.

Even if he could get someone from town in to help, chances were it'd only be part-time.

He had a full-time problem.

Becky was talking a blue streak in her own way, arms flying. Kayla watched, nodding, saying nothing. But there was a world of response in her animated expressions, in the way she used her eyes and moved her mouth....

He forced himself to look away.

Wielding her crayon, Becky bent over her picture, leaving Kayla free to lean toward him again. This time, he managed not to follow suit.

"Come on, Sam." Her voice cracked. "Hasn't she been through enough?"

He set his jaw. She seemed to care for Becky, he had to give her that. Just as she seemed to distrust him. Thanks to Ronnie.

"She knows me," Kayla continued. "She can talk to me. Even more to the point, she can understand when I talk to her." He could tell she fought to keep her voice low, to keep their conversation as private as she could. "I've said this all before, Sam. And it's all still true."

He said nothing.

Suddenly, she sat upright, her back ramrod straight, her blue eyes blazing. "Let's ask Becky *her* opinion."

"You're pulling my leg. She's a four-year-old."

Ignoring him, she waved to Becky and began talking as she signed. *"Your Daddy wants to know—"* Kayla eyed him for a split second.

Sam glared.

"—do you want Aunt Kayla to stay with you?"

Before he could tell her what he thought of her low-down tactic, the words were driven from his mind by Becky's shriek of pleasure. She pushed the drawing aside and threw her arms around Kayla.

Kayla hugged her in return.

The child slid from her seat, her hands moving like the wind.

"She's saying, *Can you stay?*" Kayla told him. *"Please, Aunt Kayla, can you stay?"*

Watching his daughter bounce up and down in excitement made his chest hurt.

How could he agree to go along with Kayla's idea?

His own unwanted reaction to her was bad enough. How could he risk letting her cement her relationship with the child? How could he just hand over to her everything she'd need to have the judge take his daughter away from him?

He felt that muscle in his cheek twitch again.

"Look at her," Kayla murmured, her tone neither pleading nor demanding, just daring him to see her side of things.

When he held his tongue, she added, "I'm not going anywhere, Sam. I'll be here in town for the next six weeks, until the judge makes his decision. Let me stay at the ranch."

He swallowed hard.

Okay, maybe that would be the best thing for Becky right now.

He wanted the best for his daughter, no matter what.

But there was no way he wanted to live in the same house with this woman. Not for *any* length of time.

"Let me stay," she urged again. "For Becky's sake."

Chapter Six

In the backyard, Sam tossed another bag of feed into the metal storage shed he used for extra stock and wiped away the sweat running down his forehead. After a morning with Kayla Ward, he'd felt the need to come out here and work off some of his aggression. It had taken all afternoon, and he wasn't sure he'd succeeded yet. Their showdown at the Double S had about pushed him to his limits.

Jack ambled over from the barn. "Tough day?"

Sam exhaled heavily. "You know it."

"Looks like you've got yourself some company."

"Yeah," he growled. Briefly, he filled Jack in on what had happened in court that morning. "The woman refuses to take no for an answer. I shouldn't have backed down. Wouldn't have, if only she hadn't played her trump card."

"Becky."

"Uh-huh."

"Considering the situation…"

"No need to be roundabout with it, Jack. I'm stuck, all right."

"Having her here might help your case in the long run. Buy you some time to get her to drop the idea of custody."

"Yeah, I thought of that. And to find out just what lies Ronnie told her." Ronnie had to be the one who'd convinced Kayla he wasn't fit to be a father to his own child.

"You think your ex fed her a load of bull about you?"

Sam laughed bitterly. Jack hadn't been around in Ronnie's day. Even if he had been, Sam would have kept those kinds of troubles to himself. He hefted another bag of feed. "See this, Jack? A drop in the bucket compared to the amount of bull she slung around here." He tossed the bag into the shed.

Maybe he could also buy enough time to defend himself against those lies. Although what Kayla thought about him, he didn't much care.

What Ronnie had said to him—and *didn't* say—bothered him a lot more. Not for the first time, he cursed her to hell and back. "She never even told me about the baby," he muttered.

"Being deaf?"

"Being born. Or even about her being pregnant before she left, for that matter."

Jack's jaw dropped.

Sam nodded grimly. What else was there to say?

He'd contacted Ronnie after she had left, but she'd turned down any of his last-ditch attempts to work things out. In these past two days, he'd realized why. She'd been more concerned about keeping him from finding out they were going to have a child. She'd succeeded in that, all right. And in making him what he was at this moment—a man who couldn't talk to his own daughter.

A fact Kayla hadn't hesitated to tell the judge that

morning. He wondered why she hadn't tossed in something about his not contacting the child.

The thought made him freeze in place. *Of course.* She believed he'd known about the baby all along. She would also believe whatever Ronnie had told her about why he'd never kept in touch.

Once again, his ex had twisted the truth to put him in a bad light.

Across the yard, the child played a game of her own with some empty wire spools and a couple pieces of twine.

He'd seen her joyful reaction to her reunion with Kayla, the even more ecstatic response to the idea of having her aunt come to stay. Both sights had driven a stake into his heart. Kayla's words had hammered it home.

Let me stay. For Becky's sake.

That did it. He hadn't had it in him to go on refusing her.

"Sam?"

Hearing her voice again so unexpectedly felt like another whack at the stake. "Yeah," he yelled. "Out back." He dropped the last bag of feed onto the pile.

"So," he said to Jack, "looks like I've got myself a houseguest. For a while."

"Think I'll head over to the bunkhouse."

"Going lily-livered on me?"

They both laughed.

Jack had barely made his exit when Kayla appeared around the corner of the shed.

She had changed from her chinos and silky shirt to a soft green T-shirt, faded jeans and tennis shoes. The transformation didn't do a thing to make her less of a spit-shine city girl. But it did make her seem more approachable.

Too bad he didn't plan to get within a hundred yards of her.

When she started across the space toward him, his shoulders instinctively drew back. Before she could reach him, her movement must have caught Becky's eye. The child looked up, saw her aunt and headed that way, running welcome interference. Kayla stopped to wrap her arms around the girl.

After one quick gesture, Kayla started toward him again. Unfortunately, Becky ran back to her makeshift toys, removing any barrier he might have relied on.

"Thanks for the use of the computer."

Her voice sounded stiff. *Good.* The last thing he needed was her getting comfortable around here. Especially since she was making him more uncomfortable than he wanted to admit.

He dug around in his mind for something to say. "You get everything taken care of?"

She nodded as if she had a crick in her neck.

"I made a few phone calls, changed a couple of appointments. And this morning," she added, "I arranged to have a box of clothes sent overnight to me…since I'll be here for a while."

As if he needed the reminder.

If she was anything like his ex, that box would come loaded down with clothes. And cosmetics, of course. Living with Ronnie had given him an up-close view of what a woman could make of herself if she wanted to.

He didn't care about Kayla's looks.

Well, he couldn't honestly say that. But he'd bet anything her honey-brown hair and pink lips had some help from modern science, too. Still, he couldn't help noticing yet again she was one heck of a looker.

"Are you planning to stay out here much longer?" She ran her gaze over him, and he could just see her mind setting to work, ticking items off a list that judged him from head to toe. Took a lot of nerve.

Deliberately he moved forward. Let her get a *real* look at him. That ought to scare her off. She probably went out with men who hadn't done a day's labor in their lives and wore three-piece suits to ball games. "What's the matter?" he asked. "Never seen good, honest sweat before?"

"Not so much of it." She eyed him coolly. "At least, not outside a gym."

That unruffled, self-possessed expression had him reaching for the shirt he'd left hanging from a fence post earlier. He'd intended to get fully buttoned up again, but some contrary reaction deep inside instead made him grab the shirt and sling it across one shoulder. "Welcome to my world."

"Oh?" She wrinkled her nose. "In your world, do people shower before meals?"

"That depends how much they need one."

Eyebrows up, she ran her gaze over him again.

"Yeah, yeah," he said. "I get it." When she turned back toward the house, he fell into step beside her. "That means you're doing supper?"

"If I can find something to pull together for a meal. There were only the basics in the fridge when I made breakfast this morning, and I used up quite a bit of those."

"Freezer's fully stocked."

She nodded. "We probably should have stopped at the store while we were in town. I can go tomorrow, if needed. Meanwhile, I'll check out the freezer and see what I can do."

"Then I'll get showered up." He took the three steps of the back porch in one long stride. "And I'll be back to check *you* out, lady," he muttered under his breath as he entered the kitchen. "You can be sure of that."

So much for his earlier thought about her not getting comfortable. She seemed to be slipping right into his household in a way he didn't care for. Even less did he like the wicked ideas she'd triggered in him. This whole situation had thrown his reactions out of whack. His good judgment, too.

With every minute that passed, he felt a growing, gut-wrenching certainty that agreeing to let her stay here had been one huge mistake.

THE SOUND OF SAM'S BOOTS on the wooden stairs in the living room sent Kayla into overdrive.

She had begun to set places at the round pine table in the middle of the kitchen, but her movements had slowed almost to a crawl even as her thoughts raced.

Her mind kept drifting back to a short time before, when she'd stood out in the yard talking to Sam.

Gawking at Sam, to be more precise.

She'd never known the sight of a man sweating could look so…intriguing. Or maybe it was the view of him without his shirt, the play of muscles beneath his tanned skin. In any case, she could barely think straight as she stared from the damp-curled hair at his forehead to his old, scuffed cowboy boots and at every dust-covered part in between.

After he'd left the yard, she had brought Becky into the house and settled her on a couch with her dolls. Then she had gone back into the kitchen to get dinner ready. First, though, she'd had to sit on one of those wooden chairs at the table for a few minutes, trying to pull herself together.

She had succeeded. Admirably.

Or so she thought—until Sam entered the kitchen, looking freshly shaved and showered and smelling like good, clean soap.

She almost fell apart again. Quickly, she moved to finish setting the table. The sound of the dishes clattering more loudly than she'd expected made her jump.

Time for her to calm down. She took a deep breath and said, "Should I set a place for your mother?"

He shook his head. "She said she'll be down in the morning."

"Okay." How would his mother like the idea of another woman in her kitchen? Mentally, she shrugged. There wasn't anything she could do about that. "I pulled a noodle casserole from the freezer," she continued, "and just threw together a salad from the greens in the crisper."

"Uh-huh."

"You were right, the freezer is well-stocked. I'm going to need to buy a few perishables, though. And I'm wondering—"

"I'll leave you some cash on the table in the morning."

He opened the dishwasher and began transferring its contents into the cabinets lining the wall above.

She frowned. "It wasn't the money I was asking about."

"It's my house. I'll pay for the food, no questions about it."

No further discussion, either, evidently.

Why was she ready to argue the point? A nanny from

a child care service wouldn't pay for groceries, either. At least his abrupt statement had helped bring her back to her cool, rational self.

"My question," she said with emphasis, "would have been, where do you—or your mother—shop for groceries?"

"And there's an easy answer to that one, since there's only one market in town. Harley's General. On the main street. We passed it on the way to the Double S."

"The wooden storefront with the striped awning?" At his nod, she added, "I remember it. Becky and I will take a trip there tomorrow morning." When he didn't respond, she said, "I'll take the casserole out of the oven while you let Becky know it's time to eat."

"I'll handle the casserole." He crossed in front of her, nearly brushing against her in his apparent haste to get to the oven.

Raising her brows, she stared at his back and somehow managed to swallow her response. But by the time she returned to the kitchen, Becky in tow, she knew eating would be next to impossible if she had to keep biting her tongue.

Chapter Seven

Luckily, once the three of them were seated at the dinner table, Becky began chattering away. Kayla voiced everything so Sam could follow the conversation.

She might as well not have bothered.

He seemed more interested in his dinner and rarely looked away from his plate for very long. When he did glance up, he never once made eye contact with either of them. As the meal went on, Kayla grew more concerned. And more irritated.

After Becky quieted down and focused on her own plate, Kayla turned her attention to Sam. Now, instead of wanting to hold back, she was determined to get him to talk.

"Becky needs some interaction with children her own age," she told him. "I'd like to get her involved in something fun. Maybe a swim class or arts and crafts, something that will help her burn up energy but keep her attention. Is there anything like that in town?"

It took a few seconds for his response. "Nothing I know of."

She nodded in acknowledgment. "I'll do a little research tomorrow, see what I can find. Do you have any recommendations about where to start?"

"No."

"Are there any of your neighbors who might know about classes?"

"I doubt it."

He seemed reluctant to cooperate with her on anything to do with Becky. How could he be so unconcerned about her?

Kayla looked away. His lack of enthusiasm wouldn't stop her from doing what she could, on her own if she had to. Becky wouldn't be here very long, but still, she was a friendly child who liked to play with others.

Besides, interacting with the locals would provide Kayla with an opening she desperately needed.

Sam and Ellamae might have lowered their voices in the courtroom that morning, but out in the hallway, Kayla had been able to pick up on the woman's caution to Sam.

The judge wanted Sam and Becky to get comfortable with one another, and for the judge's spies in town to see that and report back to him.

Well, Kayla would make darned sure those spies got a good eyeful of just how well *she* got along with her niece.

The thought of almost using Becky this way gave her a momentary pang of conscience. She couldn't let that stop her. All her efforts were for her niece's benefit. Her only goal was to take care of Becky. To do that, she would have to please the judge so he would let her take her niece home again.

If Sam didn't want to cooperate with her idea to find playmates for Becky, that could only work in *her* favor. She kept her smile and voice determinedly offhand. "I'll check at Town Hall or with your Chamber of Commerce. Someone will know about summer activities."

"It's a small town."

"Yes. I'm aware of that." Ellamae had warned *her* that morning, too. "But there should at least be some type of arts and crafts available. Or maybe a reading club at the library. They might even have a weekly story hour."

"She can't hear."

Kayla swallowed her sigh. His response didn't surprise her. It couldn't make her angry, either. Unfortunately, she'd seen plenty of people react just as he had done. People who had been around deaf children a lot longer than Sam had, and who should have understood without needing an explanation.

She looked at him. "Sam. If a librarian reads a story, I can interpret it for Becky. How do you think she'll manage when she goes to school? She'll be provided with an interpreter."

Her niece wouldn't be attending school in Flagman's Folly. But by not mentioning that little detail, Kayla might lull him into thinking he had a chance to keep Becky here. Into thinking Kayla wouldn't give him much trouble at all. "She'll be in a mainstream class with a hearing teacher, hearing students and the interpreter. Since that's the case, a story hour or some kind of summer class would be perfect right now, to get her ready for the experience."

"The other kids…" He trailed off.

"Will love her," she assured him. "And kids pick up quickly. I'll have time to teach them enough basic sign to let them learn to talk with Becky."

He shrugged and turned abruptly back to his dinner.

His behavior infuriated her. Is this how he had acted when he was with Becky and his mother the first day? Had he attempted to talk with his daughter? Or even to interact with her?

Kayla wiped her mouth carefully with her napkin, placed the napkin carefully in her lap and turned to Sam. "How was your dinner?"

"Fine."

"It ought to have been, I guess, since it was mostly your mother's cooking."

"Yeah."

"She's a good cook."

"Uh-huh."

"And a good mother and grandmother."

"Yeah, sure." Unsmiling, he looked toward her.

"What about *you?*" she asked, purposely adding emphasis to the last word.

"Am I a good cook?" He kept his tone light, but his eyes turned a cold gray as he locked gazes with her.

Her mouth went dry. She despised herself for having to clear her throat before speaking. "You know what I mean." She glanced over at her niece and found her busy making a small mound of her peas, which she hated. Kayla turned back to Sam. "Are you even *trying* to be a father to Becky? You didn't once get involved in our conversation."

He shrugged. "You two seemed to be carrying on okay."

"That's not the point."

He tossed his napkin down beside his empty plate. Then he stood, pushing his chair back so abruptly, the legs screeched against the wooden floor. "The point is," he said, "you're here to watch my child for a short time while my mother's out of commission. It's not part of your job to direct the talk at the supper table."

She opened her mouth quickly—and just as abruptly closed it again. Becky looked up, turning her head from one to the other of them, her expression quizzical.

Smiling, Kayla signed to her that dinner was over and she should go play in the living room until dessert time. She nodded, happy to abandon the peas, and slid from her chair. Kayla watched until her niece had left the room, then took a deep breath and turned back to Sam.

Becky hadn't understood what was going on.

Neither did Kayla. That flame of interest she'd felt in Sam out in the yard had been doused by a cold shower of genuine confusion. How could he have so little regard for his daughter? And how could he sit and ignore them both? If she'd ever doubted Ronnie's claims about Sam's behavior, she certainly had proof of it now.

She looked up at him. "Well, Sam," she said finally, "who else will direct the conversation around here, if I don't? You?"

"I'm not much for talking at mealtime," he said.

"I noticed that."

"Good." He shoved his chair in, leaned toward her and almost hissed, "Then I expect you won't have a problem remembering it."

SAM COULD HAVE KICKED himself. He had blurted those words in anger, hadn't really meant what he'd said. To tell the truth, he had a feeling most of his temper wasn't directed at Kayla at all.

In the living room, he watched Becky playing with her dolls. She had them lined up along the couch and sat talking to them, her fingers flying.

The sight only increased his feeling of incompetence whenever he came near her.

He would never be able to sit and have a conversation with Becky. To teach her the things daddies taught their daughters. To read her a bedtime story, tuck her in and tell her he loved her.

Maybe things would've been a whole lot different now if he and Ronnie had done some communicating of their own. If he'd known about his daughter. But the marriage had turned so bad, so quickly, life around here had fallen into a state as unproductive as two armed camps on either side of No-Man's-Land.

Maybe he could have handled things with Kayla better.

On second thought, judging by the way he'd stormed out of the kitchen after supper, maybe not.

From that direction now, he could hear Kayla clattering plates together. He hadn't given a second thought to her when he'd walked away. Just as, now, she wasn't giving even a first thought to what it would cost to replace a whole set of dishes.

Another thing she had in common with his ex.

If he didn't want a new expense to add to the long list Ronnie had left behind, he'd better do something about Kayla.

Besides, he needed to make her forget the parting shot he'd taken as he'd left the table. If she ran with his comment to the judge, he could kiss any chance of custody goodbye.

The thought left him shivering in a cold sweat.

He threw aside the newspaper he'd pretended to read and jumped to his feet.

Becky looked up, her face taking on that same bewildered expression she'd had at the supper table. He gave her what he hoped passed for a reassuring smile.

Then he marched past her and back into the kitchen.

Kayla walked toward the table, refusing to look at him, he knew. She reached for the noodle casserole.

"Let me give you a hand with that." He grabbed the dish.

"I can manage it."

"I'm sure you can. But it's my house, remember? My kitchen, too. I appreciate you doing the cooking, and I figure the least I can do is help clear up. I'm used to it."

She shot him a puzzled look that resembled Becky's, but with a lot more punch behind it. "You've had a sudden change of heart."

He forced a rueful smile. "Let's just say I found my company manners." Better to think of her that way, as a guest in his home, a *temporary* visitor. Which is exactly what she was.

Although not nearly temporary enough to suit him.

LATER THAT EVENING, KAYLA almost laughed as she thought of what Sam had said. She stood in the guest bedroom, rummaging through her overnight bag, and shook her head.

Did he really think she would fall for that line? She doubted he had any company manners. At least, she hadn't seen any evidence of them yet. No, he had something else up his fresh, clean, T-shirt sleeve.

Trying to make her forget his outburst in the kitchen, more than likely.

As if she could.

Still, she had pretended to go along with the idea, needing to keep things peaceful for Becky.

The thought of her niece made her smile. The thought of the surprise she had for her made her grin.

She had left Becky in the bathroom, brushing her teeth at the sink, eager for the bedtime story Kayla had promised her.

Hurrying across the bedroom, Kayla stepped out into the hall and almost ran into Sam. She came to a dead halt. So did he.

His gaze dropped to the object in her hand.

"What's that?"

"Just a stuffed animal." She forced herself to speak naturally to him. "It looks pretty awful, doesn't it? It's well loved." She held the toy up to show him. A small black bear, once furry but now with a worn and matted pelt, a squashed nose and only one eye. "I had it in my carry-on but forgot to tuck it in with Becky last night. I can't believe Ronnie didn't pack it up with Becky's things. It's her favorite toy. I bought it at the airport in Santa Fe the day Ronnie and I—"

Left.

She'd cut herself off, but the unspoken word hung between them, as hurtful and harsh as if she'd yelled it at the top of her lungs. Mentally kicking herself, she rushed on. "It's the state animal, Ronnie said."

"A black bear." He nodded. "I would have bought one for Becky, too. If I'd known about her."

"If you'd…?" She tried again. "What…what are you saying?"

"Plain enough. I never knew about Becky. Never even knew Ronnie was expecting."

She gasped and shook her head. How could that be possible?

But there was no missing the pain that filled his eyes.

Despite their uneasy relationship, despite all Ronnie had said about Sam, Kayla couldn't help feeling devastated by the sight. Before she could think, she reached out to him. Just short of touching his arm, she pulled her hand back. Frozen in place, she stared at him, unable to say a word.

Mixed emotions tumbled through her. Confused thoughts muddled her brain.

"But…" Again, she halted. Finally, she found her voice. For the little good it did her. "You never wanted anything to do with the baby. Ronnie told me—"

"Yeah," he interrupted in a dull tone. "I'm sure she did."

Abruptly, he turned and walked away.

She wanted to stop him, to reach out without retreating this time, to make some kind of physical contact that would ease his pain.

Instead, she did the only thing she could do. She wrapped both arms around the well-worn bear and hung on tight.

Chapter Eight

Sam paced his bedroom floor and tried to swallow his groan.

Kayla didn't believe him.

He could tell from her expression, from her halting words. From the way she'd reached out to him and then backed away as if he were something she wouldn't touch.

That same contrariness he'd felt out in the yard before supper had him wanting to reach for her, too. Dang, but this arrangement of theirs seemed nothing but a lead-in to trouble.

It had taken all he was worth to walk away from her without first tracing his fingers down the length of her silky brown hair.

And without responding to his need to unload more of the truth.

He wouldn't get anywhere with trying to talk her into giving up the idea of custody if she already held a long list of grievances against him. All the lies Ronnie had ever told about him—and there were a hell of a lot. To hear his ranch hands and the townsfolk tell it, his ex couldn't come up with a straight story if they'd handed her a slide rule. No wonder Ellamae had automatically trusted he'd never known about Becky.

Kayla, on the other hand, would believe all the stories Ronnie had made up.

Worse, Kayla had seen all the times he froze when he came near his own daughter.

Yeah, the woman sure didn't miss that.

Dumping more on her about Ronnie would only give her ammunition to use against him with the judge.

He *had* to keep custody of his daughter. Too much of her life had already been lost to him.

He left the bedroom and strode down the hall, determined to head downstairs and get outside, where he could mull things over. Having that woman in his house had done serious damage to his ability to think. But as he neared Becky's room, his steps slowed and finally stopped just outside the open door.

Inside the room, Kayla and Becky sat on the floor with a picture book spread open on the rug between them. Kayla's arms were raised, her hands skimming through the air in gestures he couldn't begin to identify. Becky knew what they meant. She sat there, entranced, with her eyes bright and her mouth stretched in a grin.

He stood there, staring, unnoticed by either of them.

Kayla's gestures grew larger, her face even more animated. And, for the first time ever, he heard his little girl laugh. The high-pitched, trilling giggle jolted hard inside his chest and made him struggle to catch his breath.

What he wouldn't give to be able to make Becky laugh like that.

His chest tightened another notch at the thought, which had turned into an almost-silent plea. The truth was, he *couldn't* give her what she so obviously needed.

At least Kayla could talk to the child—as she hadn't hesitated to rub in since the minute she'd set foot in the house. But she wouldn't be here for very much longer.

He'd see to that. The six weeks would pass before they could blink, he'd satisfy the judge's crazy requirements and Kayla would go back to Chicago.

Finally, he would have custody of Becky. And he would do what was best for his child.

He stood in the hallway, looking into the room.

An outsider in his own home.

After one last glance, he turned from the doorway, his steps surer now as he went downstairs and into the room he used as an office. Without pausing, he crossed to the old-fashioned rolltop desk in the corner and sat heavily in the swivel chair behind it.

The desk, broad and solid, had filled the corner of this room in the ranch house for four generations. The cheap, mass-produced stuff they made nowadays could never measure up to this. Most of the folks he knew agreed. No surprise then, that Manny had asked him to create the new sign for the café.

Sam never begrudged his good friend the time and effort it took to design and make the wooden plaque that now hung outside the Double S. But in his heart, he knew he'd have done the same for anyone in town. The job had given him satisfaction, an extra channel for his creative energy, a way to distract him from his problems.

It had let him make another check mark on the list of things he did to get right with the whole of Flagman's Folly.

Though he did those things to satisfy himself, to make up for the time he'd run wild as a teen, he couldn't help but wonder. Did the judge's spies ever hurry back to him with news of any of the *good* things Sam had done?

He shoved the rolltop's curved front panel up in its

track, revealing pigeonholes overflowing with papers and pamphlets and bills.

Luckily, that panel had been closed earlier when Kayla had come in to use his computer.

He looked at the pile of information he'd accumulated and thought again of Becky. Only two days since she'd come home, and he'd spent a lot of that time thinking. Had unearthed a lot of research. Had retrieved reams of data from the computer.

All that involved facts and figures.

He weighed the load of dry but critical information against the living, breathing, *laughing* little girl he'd just left upstairs.

No, he couldn't provide everything his little girl needed.

But he knew the first step he had to take toward finding someone who could.

He swiveled his chair around to face the computer on the table at his right elbow, opened his email program and started tapping the keys.

ALONE IN THE KITCHEN the next morning, Kayla paced the tiled floor.

Becky had gone outside to play on the back porch.

Sam had left the house early, even before she and Becky had woken. Downstairs, instead of the money she had expected to find, he'd left a note on the kitchen table.

Will meet you and Becky at the Double S at noon.

No, not what she had expected at all, from the stories Ronnie had told her about Sam's self-imposed isolation. His unwillingness to go far from the ranch.

He was doing this to satisfy the judge. She had to remember that.

She'd left her cell phone on the counter. When it rang, she pounced on it. At the sight of Matt Lawrence's number, her heart thumped erratically. She had talked to him the day before to give a rundown of what had happened in court. He'd had no news for her then. But now…

"Just checking in, Kayla. I'm sorry to say we don't have anything to report yet."

She didn't know whether to feel happy or sad. In a way, she almost hoped Matt wouldn't track Ronnie down. What if she got it into her head to take Becky back again? Kayla couldn't deal with seeing her precious niece sent back and forth across the country between parents who didn't really want her.

"I know you haven't heard from Ronnie," Matt continued, "or you'd have called me. She hasn't gotten in touch with your parents, either?"

"No."

"And no contact with Lianne?"

"No. Ronnie never keeps in touch with her." Ronnie had never learned to sign with Lianne. She knew only the basics of communicating with Becky. "She doesn't contact me very often, either," Kayla told him. "She usually just leaves messages with my mom and dad."

"All right, maybe she'll get around to doing that. Meanwhile, we're following up on the leads you gave us." Kayla hadn't known much to tell him about Ronnie's private life, but she had managed to dredge up a couple of men's names from memory. "Let me know if you hear anything at all."

"I will, Matt. Thanks. And I should have asked already—how is Kerry?"

Matt's wife, an art teacher, had missed the last few weeks of school when she'd gone on maternity leave.

"Getting cranky," he told her. "She's not happy with the enforced bed rest."

Just what Sam had said about his mother. "Well, she's got to take care of that baby. Say hi for me and let her know I'll see her as soon as I get back to Chicago."

There was a long pause, as if they were each wondering just when that would be.

"Sure," Matt said finally. "Before we hang up, though, is there anything else I can do?"

Kayla bit her lip. He'd asked her already about doing a background check on Sam, and she had wanted to hold off for Ronnie's sake. But time was passing, and though she planned to talk with Sam's mother and friends and any of his neighbors she could, who knew if they'd be willing to tell her anything. She took a deep breath.

"I think it's time to go ahead with that check on Sam. But, please, Matt, make sure it's discreet." If the judge found out she was trying to go around his orders, she might never get custody of Becky. "And let me know if you hear anything about Ronnie. I'll do the same."

She ended the call and jumped when a noise sounded from the direction of the living room. Matt's mother stared at her from the archway. With a pang of guilt, Kayla wondered how long the woman had been there.

Though she had crutches propped under each arm, Sam's mother leaned awkwardly against the door frame. Kayla had only gotten a glimpse of her when Sam escorted her into the house the other night. A petite woman in her early sixties with Sam's dark hair shot with silver, bright blue eyes and a flawless complexion. Kayla suspected the lines etched around her eyes were caused by pain.

Her heart went out to the woman.

Crossing the room quickly, she pulled a chair away from the kitchen table. "Please sit down, Mrs. Robertson."

"Sharleen," the woman corrected with a Southern twang much softer than Judge Baylor's. She lowered herself into the chair.

"Why didn't you call me?" Kayla asked. "I could have helped you with the stairs."

"Thought I could handle them myself." She sighed heavily. "Thought wrong, I guess."

"Becky and I just finished breakfast. Can I get you something? I'd have brought you up a tray, but Sam told me last night you didn't want anything in your room this morning."

"No. I'd planned to come downstairs. Just not quite this late."

"We had pancakes, and I've got batter left." She opened the refrigerator door. "It'll just take me a minute to make some."

"If you don't mind."

"Not at all."

Kayla got to work, heating up the skillet again, setting a place at the table and pouring a glass of orange juice. It didn't take long at all before she had a plateful of pancakes ready.

"Hope these are the way you like them." She smiled as she set the plate in front of Sharleen. "I'm sure it's a little awkward having another woman cooking in your kitchen."

"When it's a woman who's out to make trouble for my family, it is." The twang had disappeared completely. Sharleen Robertson's voice and blue eyes had turned

colder than the container of orange juice Kayla had just
picked up to return to the refrigerator.

She set the juice carefully on the shelf, then closed
the door quietly. She turned to the table again. "I'm not
here to make trouble," she said. "Only to do what's right
for Becky."

"Sam wants that, too, you know."

"I *don't* know that, for sure." She swallowed hard,
but curiosity won out. Against her better judgment, she
blurted, "He said he didn't even know about Becky."

"That's right. Neither of us did. We hadn't heard a
thing about that little girl until Ronnie brought her here
and left her."

Kayla wondered. Maybe Sharleen had known nothing, but Sam...? How could she believe him, against all
Ronnie's claims?

The sound of a dog's bark distracted her. The noise
had come from the backyard.

She moved over to the screen door and saw Becky
outside with one of the ranch animals, a puppy. He
looked like a Labrador-shepherd mix. His body and
nose were dark, his face tan. A large dark patch of fur
completely circled one eye, giving him a permanently
startled expression.

Kayla smiled.

She looked over at Sharleen, who had started in on
the plate of pancakes. "I'll be right outside with Becky
if you need something," she said.

Out on the porch, she sank to the top step.

When Becky saw her, she snapped her fingers and
pointed. *Dog.* She covered her eye with her hand.
Pirate.

Kayla laughed. A good name for the little pup. And
so nice for Becky to have a friend.

Keeping a watch on the clock, she let the two play together. After a while, she looked through the screen door again and found the kitchen empty. Sharleen must have made her way into the living room or up the stairs again without help.

As the morning wore on, Kayla glanced more and more often at the time. She wanted to be in town at the Double S long before Sam arrived.

It might take a while to get Becky cleaned up. She and Pirate had spent their time running back and forth across the yard and tramping around the barn.

Kayla waved Becky over to her.

The sooner they got to the café, the more opportunity she would have to talk to Dori. To find out what the woman could tell her about Sam. Because, obviously, Sharleen Robertson wouldn't say anything but good about her son.

Much as Kayla understood that, she felt frustrated by it, too.

Somehow, she'd have to find *someone* who would open up to her about Sam.

As she neared the Double S, Kayla eased her foot off the gas pedal. Slowing to a crawl, she almost unwillingly glanced toward the front of the building at the sign Sam had made. Creative and quirky and wonderful. All things that the man himself was not.

From the backseat, Becky squealed. She had seen the café, too. In the rearview mirror, Kayla saw her tap the fingertips of her right hand against the palm of her left. Her eyebrows climbed toward her hairline.

"Cookie?" Becky asked.

And the message said, obviously, she wanted one.

"We had all those sweet pancakes at breakfast this

morning," Kayla told her, signing the sentence in the language her niece would understand.

And Becky did. Still, she ran those same fingertips she'd used to sign *cookie* down the length of her T-shirt. *"Hungry."* And she grinned.

Kayla rolled her eyes. She had always made it a point not to spoil the child. Not too much, anyway. But Becky sure knew what buttons to push.

Yet it had been a long while since breakfast. And Becky had expended a lot of energy playing with Pirate that morning.

Besides, the cookie would keep Becky occupied while Kayla talked with Dori.

After parking the car, she released Becky from her booster seat and ushered her through the doorway of the Double S.

Most of the tables and booths in the café were filled with customers. Becky ran ahead to the dessert case. Kayla crossed to the counter at the rear of the room. Maybe she should have come earlier, instead of letting Becky and Pirate have their fun. Dori might not have a chance to chat immediately, and Kayla would risk Sam walking in during the middle of their conversation.

Fortunately, after just a few minutes, Dori bustled across the room toward them. "Good morning. You've come for more of my sweets, yes?"

Kayla laughed. "Since Becky has her nose nearly glued to the dessert case, I guess I have to admit she has, at least."

"Very good." Briskly, Dora turned to pour a cup of tea for Kayla. "I am happy to see you."

She soon settled Becky on the stool next to Kayla's with a chocolate-chunk cookie and a glass of milk in front of her. "Sam is at his ranch this morning, I'm sure. A very hard worker, that man."

"Yes." Kayla leaned forward eagerly. Dori couldn't have given her a better opening. "He doesn't seem to leave the ranch very much at all."

"Now he does, more than he did before. But there was a time..." Dori's eyes looked sad, her face grave.

"You mean...?"

"When he would not come in to town at all. When he wouldn't talk to anyone, after his wife went away."

Kayla swallowed a groan. This was not where she'd expected the conversation to go. Worse, thinking of that time only reminded her how much Sam resented her for helping Ronnie. How much he hated her for wanting to take Becky from him now. She pushed the thoughts away. She should be focusing on what she needed to do to accomplish just that, not on how Sam felt about her.

"But if he never bothered to spend any time with his wife..." At Dori's incredulous expression, she faltered.

"What is this, not bother? He works hard on his ranch from morning to night. For his wife. And now, for his little girl."

They both looked at Becky, who had pushed hard against the counter to make her seat swivel in a circle.

"I know," Kayla said, "but—"

"He's a good provider," Dori interrupted, nodding emphatically. "Like my Manny. Is that not right?" She directed the question to the person who had just slid onto the stool on the other side of Kayla's.

Kayla turned quickly to find Ellamae, the court clerk, looking at her.

"If you're talking about Sam Robertson, Dori, you're one hundred percent right. Now he's grown-up and gotten over his teenager ways, you couldn't find a better daddy this side of the Mississippi."

So Ellamae was fighting her, too, in her own way. She was probably here this morning directly from the judge's courtroom, trying to find out anything she could to help Sam.

The two women began an intense discussion about a new item on the menu.

Kayla took a deep breath and let it out. Of course these women would support Sam. He'd probably deceived everyone in town. They wouldn't know about all the things Ronnie had said, about the way Sam had treated Ronnie and rejected Becky, about all Sam's lies.

Look at that story he had told about not even knowing he'd had a child. No matter how Sharleen defended him, Kayla couldn't believe that. Ronnie had contacted Sam repeatedly, hoping he would want to get in touch with his daughter. Finally, after years of no response, she had stopped trying.

Yet, knowing all that, Kayla had let herself get swept up in thinking crazy thoughts about him yesterday afternoon. Then she had almost let herself reach out in sympathy last night. She'd come so close to falling for that hurt look in his gray eyes.

Her thoughts wavered just as her words had faltered at Dori's disbelief. Had Sam really tricked everyone into thinking he was so wonderful?

Or had Kayla been the one deceived—by Ronnie?

Before she could even begin to recover from that shocking thought, Becky cried out. Kayla recognized it as a sound of happiness.

It wasn't Becky's cry or Ellamae's satisfied nod, but

the thud of boots on the hardwood floor of the Double S that made Kayla's spine stiffen.

Slowly, as Becky had done, she swiveled her own stool to face the room behind them.

Heading across the café came the one person she had feared it would be.

Sam.

Beside her, Becky tapped her thumb against her forehead, then waved her hands palm up in the air. She made the signs over and over again. The words rang in Kayla's head as clearly as if Becky had spoken them.

"Daddy's here. Daddy's here. Daddy's here."

The sight of her niece's elated grin nearly broke Kayla's heart.

She forced her gaze to the other side of the room again, only to see Sam rapidly closing the space between them. Unable to stop herself, she found herself meeting his eyes. A tiny shiver ran through her, but when she tried to look away again, she couldn't.

If Sam planned to stay home from working on his ranch very often, they could be spending a lot of tension-filled time together.

Six weeks suddenly seemed an eternity.

She wondered if she would survive them.

Chapter Nine

For some reason, it took all Sam's willpower to cross the room to the women on the other side. He felt as though he was trying to forge a raging river. Just which of the four females over there would throw him a rope?

All of them, it looked like—although Kayla would probably then hog-tie him with it and drop him in deep water.

Why not? He was already in way over his head with this whole situation. He wanted her gone.

A quick glance at Becky almost made him trip over his own boots. Suddenly, he felt the urge to pick her up off that stool and give her a great big hug. But he held back, afraid of frightening her. He was a stranger she'd met only a couple of days ago.

Thanks to his ex.

Forcing the bitter thought away, he swept the hand holding his Stetson wide in greeting and gave them all a small bow. "Morning, ladies."

"Morning," Ellamae said with a grin.

Dori frowned at him, her eyes nearly squinted shut. "Sam, you're never here in the mornings. Is your mama all right? Is there something wrong on your ranch?"

There were lots of things wrong at his ranch. Things he didn't want to think about right now. But the biggest problem was right here at the Double S. And he was looking right at her.

Again, he needed some willpower to get him through. When he could finally tear his gaze from Kayla's sparkling blue eyes, he smiled at Dori.

"No, Mom's okay. Everything's fine. Just here for some lunch. And then after, I reckon I should show Kayla and Becky some of the sights around town."

Dori clapped her hands. "What a good idea, Sam."

Ellamae snickered.

He would shoot her a look, but she'd probably give him a shot in the arm in return. Getting what he deserved for rude behavior was more than he wanted to handle in front of his daughter.

Not to mention, in front of Kayla.

She sat watching him still, and her unblinking focus had started to do something strange to him. Had made him feel even more unsteady, as if the undertow of that deep water tugged at him. Or as if that rope he'd wondered about had just been given a mighty yank. Whatever the cause, he felt…funny.

And not in a good way.

To cover his confusion, he reached out and plopped the Stetson on Becky's head.

She gave her little trilling giggle, same as she'd done last night when he'd stood outside her bedroom. Again, it rocked him. His breath caught in his chest.

This time, *he'd* made her laugh.

Judging by the stunned look on Kayla's face, Becky's reaction had hit her hard, too. He'd have thought she'd be used to it.

The reminder that she had seen everything of his daughter's life, while he'd seen nothing, left him struggling not to glare at her in front of the other two women.

Silently, he vowed to get this situation resolved right quick.

That barbecue Judge Baylor had harped on might do the job. Kayla could make sure Becky behaved, while he spent his time making a good impression on Judge Baylor. Letting the man see that he had the means to take care of his child. That Becky needed to stay with her daddy.

Meanwhile, today, he would show his little girl off to all the fine citizens of Flagman's Folly. If Ellamae had spoken the truth, then he'd see to it every one of the judge's spies got back to the man with a good report.

Things were looking up.

He didn't have to force himself to grin at Kayla. "Well, how about it?" he asked. "Why don't we have some lunch and then get our tour started?"

The expression on her face could have dropped a coyote in its tracks from across a half acre.

KAYLA COULD BARELY RECALL what she had ordered from the menu at the Double S. She'd eaten her lunch while in a near daze and, even as she followed Sam and Becky from the café, she had trouble coming back to the present.

She couldn't seem to forget the look on Sam's face when he'd put his cowboy hat on Becky's head and heard her laugh.

The wistfulness in his eyes had started a hollow ache in her chest, and the sensation hadn't gone away yet. She had a bad feeling it was somehow connected to her heart breaking.

She needed to do something to save herself. And Becky.

"Let's leave the car and the pickup here," he said as they stood outside the café. "We'll do the length of Signal Street, but I have to say, it won't take very long to walk it."

"Oh?" she asked, forcing a cool tone. "Even so, I'm surprised you're taking the time away from your ranch to give us a tour. Ronnie once told me you were never free to do anything with her."

He looked taken aback by her response. What he *should* have realized was, she had just pointed out something she could use against him with the judge. A father who would never have time for his daughter. Guilt warred with elation over this, and to her annoyance, the decision came to a close call. Elation finally won.

Becky skipped down the street ahead of them. Kayla and Sam fell into step behind her. She had thought he would ignore her previous statement, but to her surprise, he replied.

"Kind of hard to go on tours when I normally leave the house early and get back late."

"Yes, I'm sure that's true." Point number two, no matter what Dori and Ellamae thought.

At this rate, she'd have enough to go to the judge in no time.

Before he could have a chance to figure that out, she asked, "Just how did Flagman's Folly get its name?"

He looked at her for a long while, as if wary of the change of subject. Or as if, for some reason, he felt reluctant to tell her.

At last, he said, "Back a century or so ago, there wasn't a town here, just a small crossroad station in the middle of nowhere. Trains pulled in for refueling and picking up passengers. The flagman stationed here had the job of signaling to make sure two trains didn't try to come in at the same time."

"And something happened?"

Sam laughed. "Yeah, something happened. The flagman was so busy making his moves on a waiting passenger, he messed up. And the trains collided."

Kayla gasped. "Were there many hurt?"

"No one, fortunately. The first train was slowed to a crawl getting ready to pick up passengers, and the second was a freighter with only the crew aboard."

"The flagman got off lucky."

"*Real* lucky."

At the amusement in his tone, she looked at him.

"As it turned out," he explained, "the man up and married the lady he'd been sweet-talking."

She shook her head in disgust. "Well, *that* was a lot more than he deserved."

"You could be right. The woman came from money and he was just a down-and-out bum until he got the job with the railroad." He tilted his head, and she could see his eyes twinkling beneath the brim of his hat, but he didn't say anything else.

Her heart thumped. Not only were they having a normal, peaceful conversation, Sam was teasing her, almost flirting with her.

"All right," she said after they had walked several yards down the street and he still said nothing. "I give up. What's the punch line?"

He grinned. "Those were my great-grandparents. They wound up settling here and, after a few others came along to join them, the town was incorporated. They named it *and* the main street from their story. You might say I have a vested interest in the place."

Or I might say you come from a long line of bums.
What would that do to their nice conversation?

The story of his family history made Kayla recall what Ellamae had said about Sam's "teenager ways." Something she would have to look into at a later date— and let Matt know. Maybe Sam had inherited the flag-man's incompetence as well as his genes.

And maybe, in that, she'd find point number three for the judge.

As Becky neared the next building, she slowed.

The day had gotten overly warm, with the humidity high and the temperature now at ninety-eight, according to a thermometer hanging in the sunny front window of Lou's Barbershop. Good thing Kayla had remembered to ask Lianne to throw several pairs of shorts into the boxes of clothing she'd sent.

Through the plate-glass window, one of the barbers, a gray-haired man in an old-fashioned long white apron, saw Kayla looking at the thermostat. When he noticed Becky beside her, a smile touched his face. He waved at her, and she grinned and waved back. He came to the open front door of the shop.

"Well, hey, Sam. Looks like you got yourself some company."

"Sure have." Sam introduced Becky then, after a pause, Kayla.

Lou made an instant hit with Becky when he pulled an orange lollipop out of his apron pocket.

Kayla tried not to shake her head. More sweets. Catching her niece's eye, she put her finger near her chin, then gestured with her upraised palms. *"What do you say?"*

In one swift movement, Becky raised her hand to her mouth and pulled it outward.

"Thank you," Kayla voiced for her.

"Anytime." Lou smiled.

They stopped next at the hardware and feed store.

Sam went about his job with a vengeance, she noticed, introducing Becky to everyone he knew—which seemed to be every single person they came across. As an afterthought, almost, he would remember to mention Kayla.

She decided to let that pass. For now.

At the small department store, she looked through the packages of curtains, searching for a set for the window in Becky's guest room. Which reminded her...

"Sam," she said.

He turned from his inspection of a display of window hardware.

"The headboard of the bed Becky's using. I told you I'd never seen a design like that before. Did you make it?"

He hesitated, looking away, as if he didn't want to answer the question. She couldn't understand why.

Finally, he nodded. "Yeah."

"You do beautiful work."

"I try." The words came out grudgingly.

She shrugged. If the man didn't want compliments, she'd keep them to herself in future. She selected a set of curtains in a bright floral print that would pick up the colors in the throw rugs. "I'm ready to check out."

When Becky came up beside them, Kayla held out the package to her.

Becky raised her brows and put her hand flat on her chest.

"Mine?" Kayla voiced for Sam. She nodded.

Becky took the package and ran toward the cashier at the front of the store.

"Hers?" Sam asked. "Becky's room already has curtains."

"I thought I'd buy something to make it a little more girlish in there."

"You don't need to be buying her anything."

"I want to."

"She's my child. Any buying that gets done around here, I'll do it." He turned on his heel and strode off in Becky's wake.

Kayla stood there a moment, puzzled by his strong reaction to her offer. She shrugged again. So, he didn't like his daughter to have gifts, even when they were bought by someone else.

What would the judge think about that?

THEY WORKED THEIR WAY back down the other side of the street, through the post office and the volunteer firefighter station, in the same fashion. With Sam still barely remembering to introduce her along with Becky. By that time, Kayla's previous irritation at his slights, compounded by the rejection of her gift, had worked itself up to a steady simmer. A good soak-down with one of the fire hoses might have done her some good.

Without that, the next snub from Sam would probably make her boil over. In a very polite way, of course.

They had reached Town Hall again, where Becky jogged up the path to the front steps, climbed them and jumped down. She proceeded to play this game as they stood watching.

"We'd better head back after this," Sam said. "You were planning on stopping at Harley's, right? I'll go with you. It's about time to start stocking up for that barbecue the judge invited himself to."

The barbecue. "Yes, I need to pick up a few things at the store," she said, her voice shaking.

She had hoped Sam would forget all about the judge's comment. The idea of the barbecue worried her more than she wanted to admit. That day in court, she had seen for herself how the judge seemed to favor the local boy and had heard how strongly he felt about Becky being part of the history of Flagman's Folly. Now that Sam had shared his story, she understood the judge's words. She could almost go along with them. Becky *did* have strong ties to the town. And Flagman's Folly appeared to be a nice place filled with friendly people.

Weighed against all this, could her efforts to rack up points against Sam be worthless?

On the day of the barbecue, would the judge take one look at Becky on that big, open ranch—the ranch she had the right to one day inherit—and decide that being brought up there would be in the child's best interests?

Kayla clenched her hands at her sides. This defeatist mind-set wouldn't help her, and she had to get rid of it now.

Dropping her attitude toward Sam was a different story.

Fighting to keep her voice steady, she continued, "I'm not sure about the shopping list I made. It was hard to figure out what to cook when I'll never be sure what time you'll be in for dinner."

"Ranchers work long hours." He frowned. "And I'm not used to having to report in with my schedule."

"So Ronnie told me."

He stopped and turned to her, looking suddenly as hot under the collar as she felt. "Do you have to bring that 'Ronnie told me' into every conversation?"

She shrugged. "Just making a point."

"Yeah, a point to remind me you don't know what you're talking about."

"Really?" Suddenly, Sam's series of backhanded insults and her own memory of what had happened in the courtroom of that very building where Becky now played made her even more annoyed. The knowledge of what could happen there in the next few weeks pushed her past the boiling stage. "I do know what I'm talking about, which happens to be a lot more than you think. Enough that I could march right in to your good-old-boy judge with it, and he would give me custody of Becky in a New York minute."

"All right," he said, his teeth clenched. He turned to face her and leaned down to meet her eyes. "You got something like that you're sitting on, quit flapping your wings like a brood hen who's just caught a javelina in the henhouse, and say whatever you've got to say."

"Or what? You'll hit me?" Kayla demanded. "Just like you did Ronnie? Well—"

He grabbed her arm. She jerked free in outrage, feeling a momentary regret that she had blurted the question.

Sam backed away a step. "I wasn't going to hit you—"

"Oh, of course not. That's what they all say. But then, I'm not your wife, so I'm not really worried that you would—"

"Stop it," he said. "Just stop."

His face had drained of all color. His mouth hung slack for a moment, as if she had hit him in the face— literally, instead of just with her words.

"That's not what I intended to say," he continued. "I meant, I wasn't going to hit you. I just wanted you to stop saying those things. Look, I don't even know where you got that idea. Well, yeah," he contradicted himself immediately, his voice bitter. "Reckon I do. But how could you believe that?"

"Ronnie—" In spite of her eagerness to prove herself, she stopped and changed direction. "I'd seen proof, Sam. Cuts and bruises."

"*What?* When?"

"When I came here to help Ronnie leave town."

He stared at her, saying nothing, his eyes bleak and seeming unfocused. Without warning, he raised his arm and stepped toward her again.

Chapter Ten

The instant Sam saw Kayla flinch, he dropped his arm to his side.

She stood staring at him, her pupils widened to dark pools, and he realized just how much he'd frightened her.

"Listen, calm down. I'm sorry," he said, almost running the words together in his hurry to explain. "I was only going to point to Town Hall. I want you to go up to the courtroom with me to see the judge. He'll tell you the truth. Come with me, please. If I go in ahead of you," he added, fighting to keep resentment from his voice, "you might think I talked him into lying for me."

For a second, he could see her waver, torn between agreement and flight. She took a long, deep breath, then turned and walked toward Town Hall. She waved her hands in the air to Becky, who entered the building ahead of them.

He let Kayla walk ahead of him, too, and gave her plenty of room to go through the double doors into the building without crowding her. His stomach churned with both guilt and regret. Her words had torn him up inside. But he'd never meant to scare her.

Inside the courtroom, Ellamae sorted through paperwork at a small desk in the corner. Becky sat in the judge's leather swivel chair behind his huge old desk, her face all Sam could see above the surface. The judge stood beside the chair, grinning down at her. At their approach, he looked up.

Kayla's hands began moving.

"Now, young lady," he said to her, "if you're telling this little one to move, hold on, because she's got my permission to sit here."

As they watched, he swung the chair in a gentle circle, while Becky flipped her hands back and forth in the air. He waited till the chair came to a halt before turning back to them.

"Well, this is a surprise, isn't it? I didn't expect to see you two setting foot in my courtroom again so soon. What can I do for you?"

Sam hesitated, feeling like a danged fool for bringing Kayla in here. What *could* the judge do, anyhow?

Kayla didn't believe anything Sam said. Hell, she didn't even consider he'd told the truth about his own child. Why would she accept that he'd never touched his ex in anger?

"Judge—" He drew a deep breath, fighting humiliation at the thought of what he had to ask. A bead of sweat ran down his temple. For once, the overhead fan sat still, just when he needed it most. He brushed the moisture away.

"Judge Baylor," he started again, "would you tell Becky's aunt why my ex-wife was covered with cuts and bruises when she left town?"

The man's brows leveled out, straightening almost into one solid line.

From her seat in the corner, Ellamae looked up.

Beside him, Sam could see Kayla tense.

"Well, Sam," the judge drawled, looking from one

to the other of them, "it's not clear to me why I'm the one doing the telling. But you know I never mind giving out explanations." He looked at Kayla. "Your sister got herself involved in an automobile accident."

"When?" she asked.

"As I recall, this happened only a few days before she left Flagman's Folly for good."

"How do you know this?"

The judge frowned, and Sam knew she'd just crossed a line. But the man answered mildly enough. "It was common knowledge, practically soon as it happened."

"I was on the volunteer rescue," Ellamae spoke up. "She'd rolled her car into a drainage ditch between town and the ranch. Lordy, she'd gotten thrown around pretty bad. No seat belt." She shook her head.

"Fortunately," the judge added, "there were no other vehicles involved. And no other passengers."

"I—I see."

Sam heard Kayla give a deep sigh. When she turned toward him, he stiffened. She hadn't trusted in his honesty before. Nothing she could say would make up for that now.

"I'm sorry." She looked at him, her eyes shining. "I didn't know—"

"Yeah." He turned away, his step heavy. So, now she did know. The truth. It made no difference. Had he really expected it to change anything?

"Sam, please—" Her voice broke. She moved around to stand before him. "I'm truly sorry. I saw the cuts and bruises, and I only knew what Ronnie told me."

From across the room, he heard Ellamae's gasp.

Now she and the judge knew something, too, and they hadn't had to work very hard making the leap to figure it out.

"Let's just go," he said.

She gestured to Becky, and a second later he heard sneakers on the wooden floor. He was about to start out of the courtroom when the judge called his name. Freezing in place, he took a deep breath. After what seemed a long while, he turned back.

First he looked down at Becky, standing beside him.

Then he looked at Ellamae, who stared, her eyes huge.

Finally he looked at Judge Baylor, the man who'd always managed to slap him down. The man who'd never let him forget his past. And who had the power to decide his future.

The judge came around his desk and rested one hand on the wooden railing in front of the row of spectator seats. Sam eyed him, saw the man's knuckles tight on the rail and knew what to expect.

"I doubt you need me to put this in words," the judge said, in the softest voice Sam had ever heard come from him. "But I'll share it, anyway. You can't take things out on this young lady for believing what your ex-wife said. We *all* know only what others are willing to tell."

You could've heard a cactus flower drop to the floor in that room.

Even Becky, as if sensing something wrong, stood without moving.

He couldn't look at Kayla. Didn't want to see what would show in her face.

"Yeah," he said at last, staring across the courtroom again. "Gotta hand it to you, Judge." He laughed without humor. "You just summed up the whole history of my bad marriage, right there in that one short sentence."

SAM THOUGHT JUDGE BAYLOR had finished making his point.

He'd thought wrong. The man had only begun.

When he'd asked Sam to stay for a "short spell in my chambers," Kayla had looked suspiciously at them both.

He could just see the protest on her lips, the indecision in her eyes. But, finally, she simply said she would go ahead to the market with Becky, and Sam could meet them when he was done.

Unwilling to let her hear whatever else the judge wanted to say, Sam had agreed.

Now, in chambers, Judge Baylor sat back in his swivel chair and eyed Sam up and down.

He immediately flashed back more than a decade ago to the day he'd come before the judge for the first time.

Right after the night he'd set fire to the Porters' barn.

He tried to push the memory away and managed to do it—only to face the judge's double-barreled glare and to hear the man putting his own thoughts into words.

"Y'know, Sam, it's been a while since you first came into my courtroom."

"Yeah." And since then, the judge had never managed to see any good in him.

No surprise, since Sam hadn't been good for much for a while after that. The judge's warning that he'd toss him in jail and throw away the key had kicked off a rebellious streak in him that he'd never known existed.

Or maybe it had started before that....

Again, the judge voiced what Sam was thinking.

"I went easy on you back then, son, on account of your losing your daddy." He frowned and shook his head. "Too easy, perhaps. You made life hell for your mama, you know."

Sam nodded.

"But your daddy was a good friend of mine. I owed it to his memory—and to Sharleen—to allow you the chance to straighten up. I'm glad you took me up on it—" he glared again "—even if it was in your own good time."

"I was…mixed-up back then, Judge."

The man snorted. "Well, that hasn't changed much, has it? Sam, I'm not rightly sure what's going on between you and that young lady. But it's not sounding to me like you two are getting along."

"We're managing," he said as easily as he could, fighting not to break into a sweat again.

The judge looked doubtful. Was the man going to renege on the six weeks he'd allowed them and make his decision right now?

Had Sam lost his daughter already?

He wouldn't go down without a fight. He wouldn't go down at all. "We've been out around town today, having Becky meet a lot of the townsfolk."

"That's good. That's very good."

Sam elaborated, detailing the story of their travels. It seemed to appease the judge. His goal accomplished, Sam didn't waste any time getting out of the courtroom.

If only his words could have that effect on other people.

On one woman in particular.

As he headed back up Signal Street toward the market, he thought again of the judge's earlier statement. The one he'd made about people only knowing what others wanted to tell them.

And not *tell them,* Sam should have added.

Like the news Ronnie had never bothered to share with him.

Still, the judge's remark had started a question that kept circling around in Sam's brain, big and bothersome as a green-eyed horsefly.

No one knew better than he did that Ronnie couldn't shoot straight with a story if she tried. So how could he blame Kayla for falling for her sister's lies?

THE AFTERNOON HAD GOTTEN hotter and stickier as it went on. Kayla swept her hair off the back of her neck to cool it. From her seat on the top porch step, she watched Becky play with her friend, Pirate.

Sam had met them at the market as planned, though he didn't say a word about his time with Judge Baylor. In fact, he'd barely said a word about anything.

Thank goodness she'd had the rental car outside the café. She would never have made it back to the ranch if she had been forced to share Sam's pickup truck. To tell the truth, the tension between them made her want to run.

Only the knowledge that she couldn't take Becky with her kept her from leaving town altogether.

She wasn't going anywhere without her niece.

Once they arrived back at the house, the minute they unpacked the groceries, Sam had disappeared into his office, where Sharleen had set herself up at his desk, her foot propped on a stool, to use the computer.

Eager to be away from both mother and son, Kayla had followed Becky into the backyard.

Her face flushing—and not just from the heat of the day—she sagged against the porch railing.

Why had she blurted out that accusation against Sam?

Why hadn't she refused to go talk with the judge? She'd have been so much better off. Yet, that wouldn't have been fair to Sam.

Long ago, Ronnie had made her promise never to breathe a word of what she'd been told to anyone. And now that Kayla had accused him of such a terrible act, she had learned all too clearly why Ronnie had sworn her to secrecy. She had lied.

As Kayla had also accused Sam of doing.

Across the yard, Becky and Pirate disappeared behind the barn. They liked to walk—and, in the puppy's case, sniff—their way around the huge building. It always took a while.

Still agonizing over what she had done, Kayla dropped her head onto her upraised knees and groaned. How could she ever make up to Sam for the way she had treated him?

Her throat tightened as if to prevent her from saying the words aloud. Her head spun, and again, it wasn't due to the heat, but from all the thoughts whirling in her mind. Now that she had learned the truth about Ronnie's injuries, she had to question everything Ronnie had told her. Had to reexamine everything she had *thought* she'd known about Sam.

There was one thing she could swear to, though, and from her own knowledge. All Sam could think about was winning over the judge and taking Becky away from her.

If accusing him of abuse hadn't turned the judge against her, it would certainly give the man pause. Again, she worried over what had happened that afternoon in the private conference in his chambers. She should have stayed there. She should have protested the two of them going off together. Who knows what deal they might already have made?

An agreement that might be all the judge needed to decide Sam should keep custody of Becky.

All thanks to Kayla's own misinformed actions.

What was she going to do to make the judge see she was the best person to care for Becky?

From behind her came the sounds of the screen door hinges. She turned to find Sam leaning against the kitchen door frame, his slumped posture almost mimicking hers. She would have laughed, except he looked the picture of misery, and chances were if she could get her hands on a mirror, she would find she looked the same.

"Listen," he said, "I just came to tell you—" He stopped, looking past her. "What the hell is that?"

She turned quickly, her thoughts flying to Becky.

Her niece had just rounded the barn with Pirate prancing beside her.

"Call her over here," he demanded.

She looked at him in surprise. "Why? She's okay."

"Not with that mutt around her, she isn't."

"Your puppy won't hurt her. He and Becky have played together before this."

"He's not my dog. Just call her," he repeated.

She could see his frustration mounting. At the sight of the dog or at his own inability to talk to Becky, she couldn't tell. But she had to acknowledge that he'd know better than she would if there were something wrong with the dog.

She motioned Becky to come to her.

As Becky neared the porch, Pirate followed at her heels. When she started up the steps, Sam leaned over the railing to yell at the dog, waving him away. The confused pup bounded once after Becky, backed up a couple of paces, ran in a circle. At last, he stood still, his head cocked and his eyes trained adoringly on her. Sam yelled again. Pirate retreated a few feet, gave a low whine, turned to go. He paused once to glance back before finally loping away.

Becky looked just as confused as her furry friend. Her eyes wide, she snapped her fingers, then tapped her fingertips twice on her cheek. *"Dog? Home?"*

Kayla nodded.

Sam had retreated into the kitchen, and she could see him punching the keypad of the cordless phone.

Becky climbed onto the porch swing, where she had left her doll. Kayla gave the swing a push to start it moving.

A minute later, she heard Sam's voice on the phone.

"This is Sam Robertson. Tell Porter to keep his animals off my land. Including that mangy dog of his. That mutt gets anywhere near my daughter again, and I'll see Porter gets what he deserves…. Right. You do that. Word for word. He gives you any grief about delivering my message, you just let me know." He dropped the phone back onto its base.

After giving Becky another push on the swing, Kayla turned and went into the kitchen, closing the screen door softly behind her.

Sam stood with his arms folded, his hips braced against the counter, his irritation still evident. He had overreacted to seeing the puppy. But no matter what he claimed for his reason, she knew he'd jumped so quickly at the sight of the dog in an effort to protect his daughter.

And no matter how she felt about him, she had to

give him credit for that. Which she did. The trouble was, how she felt about him had started to change.

That knowledge roused more mixed emotions in her than she had time to think about right then.

She walked toward him, thought better of it and sidestepped to prop her elbow on the adjacent counter. "I didn't realize the puppy wasn't yours. I thought he belonged on the ranch."

"No."

"Well, no harm done, is there? He seems like a nice dog, always gentle with Becky."

"That's not the point. I don't want my neighbor's animals on my land."

She nodded. "That's understandable." She *didn't* understand it, but that was the most soothing thing she could think of to say right now. Hoping to distract him, and to be honest, to satisfy her blatant curiosity, she said, "When you'd come to the door before, you had started to say something."

He stretched both hands out beside him, resting them on the edges of the countertop. He looked down, scuffed one boot against the floor, cleared his throat. But he said nothing.

Her face began to flush again. "Sam, I hope you've accepted my apology for what I did. And for…" She faltered, then went on. "…for dragging the judge and Ellamae into it."

He looked up at her, his eyes narrowed. A shiver ran through her. She couldn't have explained what her own response meant if she'd tried.

"Hell of a thing we had to come to, wasn't it," he asked, "for me to prove what I'd already said?"

"I know. Sam, I really am sorry."

"Yeah, well, listen," he said, hurrying now, running

his words together just as he'd done outside Town Hall. "You want to know what I'd come outside to tell you. It's only…whatever else is going on around here, I know getting tripped up in Ronnie's tall tales isn't your fault."

"I really had no idea it wasn't true," she said, wincing even as she said the words, realizing they only helped make the uncomfortable situation worse. But she couldn't live with knowing what she had done. She swallowed hard. "Will you forgive me?"

He stared down at the toe of his boot for so long, she thought he wouldn't respond. Finally, he said, "You were getting back at me."

"No—"

"Yes. For my bad manners in not introducing you properly to folks in town."

No, she wanted to tell him. *Well, all right, maybe in part. But mostly for trying to steal my niece from me.* How could she say that, when his only reply could be, *Like you're trying to take my daughter from me?*

"Ronnie used to find ways to get back at me, too," he said.

"Sam, I—"

"I got you the truth about one of Ronnie's stories," he continued, as if she hadn't spoken. "Now let me tell you about the rest of them." He took a deep breath and let it out slowly, almost in a sigh. "I spent a lot of time a while back trying to shake off the dust of Flagman's Folly. I met Ronnie at a rodeo in Abilene and—wham!—before I knew it, we'd gotten hitched."

Kayla wanted to interrupt. She didn't need to hear this. But if it would give her a clearer picture of Sam, she couldn't afford to stop him. Besides, in her heart she wanted—needed—to know the truth. About everything.

"Sounded like a good idea at the time," he continued, "but we started fighting from day two. I don't blame her for all of it, but she didn't give anything much of a try. From the minute we came back here, things got worse. She didn't like the town, never liked living on the ranch." The skin around his eyes tightened, as if he'd winced to avoid a blow. "Tell the truth, I think she never liked me much, either."

Kayla gasped. "I can't believe that."

"Don't I know it." His voice hardened. "Seems like there's a lot around here you can't believe, until it gets shown to you. Well, I could bring you to the judge, and I did. I can't bring you to Ronnie. Maybe when you see her, you ought to put that idea to her yourself." Suddenly, he shoved against the counter, pushing himself upright. "And another thing. For the first six months of our marriage, I didn't know she even had a family. She told me she was an only child and her parents were gone."

At that news, Kayla almost staggered. She reached out, grateful for the counter beside her.

She had always admired cool, sophisticated Ronnie. Always. That image had started to crumble after their meeting with the judge earlier that day. And now, she didn't know what to think.

What Sam had said was ridiculous. "That's not true about her family. Ronnie's mom *is* gone. My mom is her stepmother. But Ronnie still has her dad—my dad. And two half sisters."

"Guess her memory's pretty patchy about that. It wasn't till she started threatening to leave that I learned about y'all."

"I can't—"

"Yeah, yeah, I know. You can't believe it." He moved forward, coming so close she had to raise her chin to look into his eyes. "Well, as we say around here, 'can't never could do nothing.' Maybe it's time you started figuring out just what you *can* believe."

Chapter Eleven

Sam pulled the pickup into the yard and parked it near the barn. Over at the house, Sharleen sat on a wooden bench on the front porch with her foot propped up on a chair and a book in her hands.

No sign of Kayla and Becky. Last he'd heard, at breakfast, they were planning on baking cookies.

It had been a long three weeks since the day he'd run off at the mouth about Ronnie. Spending most of his time in Kayla's company since then had been hard enough. They had gone into town for the Fourth of July parade. Bringing Grandma Sharleen along gave their little group the touch of a real family—and had made an already awkward situation nearly unbearable.

Leaving the supplies he'd bought in the pickup for later, he crossed the yard to the porch and leaned against the railing.

Sharleen closed her book and smiled at him. "About time you came home. Becky's been looking for you."

"She has?" For a second, his breathing hitched.

In these past weeks, he'd made some progress with Becky. Tousled her hair. Sat with her in the evenings. Sometimes handed her one doll or another. It wasn't much, but it was something. Wasn't it?

Maybe so, if she had noticed he'd gone missing that morning.

"Well," Sharleen said, "she's been prowling around here ever since noontime as if she's lost something."

"She have fun making cookies?"

She smiled. "Sure did. And Kayla made peach cobbler for supper, too."

He stared at her, his eyes narrowed. Peach, apple, cherry, it didn't matter. Cobbler was his favorite. "Was that your idea?"

"Not at all."

He wondered.

Sharleen nodded in the direction of his pickup. "Did you get everything you needed at the hardware store?"

"Yeah."

That morning, when Jack had brought up the list of supplies, Sam jumped at the chance for a trip alone. At the chance to get away from the ranch and clear his head. Too bad he hadn't succeeded at that.

Still, he'd accomplished more than just buying the supplies. "Stopped and saw the judge, too."

"That's good," she said.

Kayla wouldn't think so when she heard about it.

Becky came around the corner of the house dragging her toy-filled wagon. When she saw Sam, she grinned and waved.

He waved back.

A minute later, she bounded onto the porch, a doll and a plastic bottle in her hands. He ruffled her baby-soft blond hair.

When Sharleen patted the empty seat beside her, Becky climbed up onto the bench and settled herself with her toys. Once she'd caught the child's attention again, Sharleen cupped her hand and ran her fingertips down her stomach. "Is the baby hungry?"

Becky nodded.

Sam looked at his mother in surprise. "How did you learn that?"

"At first, just from watching. Kayla always tells me what she's saying to Becky. Then I asked her a few other words. She was nice about showing me, too."

If only things could be that easy.

Holding back a sigh of frustration, he recalled the day he'd met Kayla and Becky at the Double S for lunch. Before heading to the café, he'd stopped at the bookstore to pick up the dictionary he'd had to special-order. The book that showed the basics of sign language. The one he thumbed through night after night when everyone else in the house had gone to bed.

He had bought that dictionary feeling confident he could solve his problem on his own. But he'd soon found that talking with his hands would be a lot harder than he'd thought.

Again and again, he'd flipped through those pages, trying to figure things out, until he'd come one step away from throwing the book in the trash. Hell, like the crayoned drawings Becky had done at the Double S, he couldn't even make sense of half the book's pictures.

Sharleen frowned, squinting up at him, uncertainty in her eyes. "Sam, I can't say anything against her when it comes to Becky. She loves the child."

He couldn't deny that. But when he tried to agree, the words stuck in his throat.

"What are we going to do?" she asked. "The days are flying by."

He had told her about Judge Baylor's decision to leave Becky in joint custody for six weeks. Sam couldn't do a thing to get that changed until Ronnie surfaced. And so far, no one had seen or heard from her.

"We can't lose Becky." Sharleen looked down again at her granddaughter—the only grandchild she'd ever have.

The only child he'd ever have, too.

"We won't lose her, Mom."

"If Lloyd decides in Kayla's favor, we will."

"Don't worry, I'm working on that."

"Sam, Lloyd was a good friend to your daddy, and he's always been good to us, but I'm afraid…"

Afraid your history with the judge will hurt us.

She didn't need to say the words aloud.

"Don't worry, Mom," he told her again. "Things will be just fine."

By the time he left the porch, he had succeeded in calming her fears. He'd made her believe everything would work out.

He just wished he could believe it, too.

A few minutes later, he stood inside the ranch house, willing his feet to move forward.

Midafternoon sunlight stained the white walls of the entryway and the pine planks of the floor he'd laid himself. Putting down those planks had made him feel he'd added something solid to the land his family had owned for generations.

Well, the floor might still stand firm, but the rest of his life had fallen out from under him, thanks to the woman he could see through the kitchen doorway. The one he tried not to ogle like he was a dumb seventeen-year-old who'd never seen a real lady before.

Kayla was real, all right. No denying that, with the proof right there in—or he should say, *flowing out of*—a blue-checked sleeveless shirt that left her shoulders bare and a pair of denim shorts that showed a whole lot of leg.

Still, his fingers itched to touch her long, tanned limbs. To find out for sure if he could trust her existence. Maybe he'd get lucky and discover she'd been just a figment of his imagination.

He finally managed to tear his gaze from her. *After* he'd reached her ankles.

When he glanced up, he found she'd been watching him. Her appraising eyes and pink-blushed cheeks made him look away again in a hurry, searching for something else to focus on. But he couldn't seem to look past her altogether.

Hands. He kept his eyes on her hands. She held a striped dish towel and the drinking cup Becky had been using for her breakfasts. The bunny-covered plastic tumbler put a cold dose of reality into what could easily have turned into one hot fantasy.

Wouldn't take but a couple dozen strides, and he could have himself across both rooms and right up next to Kayla.

He stopped at the kitchen archway.

Kayla set the towel and Becky's cup on the counter. Living up to its name, the tumbler tumbled off the edge.

They lunged forward at the same time to catch it and a second later backed up just as quickly, as if they'd gotten hit with a few volts from an electric fence just from getting close. The cup bounced several times on the tile floor before rolling to a stop against the refrigerator.

Kayla didn't move.

It took an effort not to touch her as he bent down to pick up the tumbler. It took another effort not to crush the colorful plastic in his tight grip. Carefully, he placed the tumbler on the counter beside her.

"Th-thanks. Did you get everything you needed at the store?" she asked, just as Sharleen had.

He nodded. "Took care of the whole list," he confirmed.

"You were gone longer than I expected."

"I ate at the Double S at noon, then helped Manny with a couple of things."

She nodded.

Silence fell again.

He stood staring at the woman who seemed to fill all his waking moments lately—and more than a few of his sleeping ones, too. Of course, the waking ones were his own fault. Or the judge's, to tell the truth.

Thanks to Judge Baylor, all the trips to town with Becky and Kayla put Sam closer than he liked to the woman. Yet he knew he had to follow through. And not just to satisfy the judge.

To convince Kayla.

Once she learned what Sam was really like, she would accept that his daughter should stay in his care.

But this undercurrent between them—this electric-fence rush of energy he felt every time he got near her—told the truth. He should stay away from her. Far away.

Even knowing this, he couldn't seem to get his feet to move far enough to get himself out of the room. Or his mouth to stay shut long enough to stop himself from talking to her. His words ought to take care of *her* talking to *him*, though.

"Saw the judge on the way back through town, too," he said, forcing a light tone. "Told him we'd be having that barbecue he keeps asking about. Sunday."

"Sunday?" Her brows rose. "You mean *this* Sunday? Three days from now?"

"Yeah? Something wrong with that?"

"No."

But she didn't look like she meant it.

"Don't go worrying yourself over the cooking," he said in the same relaxed tone. It got easier with practice. "Jack and the boys and I will take care of barbecuing the roasts. We do it every year. Dori always handles the desserts. And the townsfolk will bring the rest."

She frowned. "You don't need me to do anything?"

Oh, hell, yeah, I do.

Clamping his jaw shut, he swallowed the words that felt all too ready to spill out. So much for relaxed and easy. "No," he said, his voice hoarse but his words final. "I don't need you to do anything at all."

On that note, he left the room.

Tried to leave Kayla behind.

He couldn't think about what he needed and wanted from the woman. Or about how regretful she'd sounded with her question. He had a lot of regrets himself, but no sense giving in to them now. He had to remember the threat she meant to him. The danger she represented. The damage she could still do to his life.

The abuse charge she'd laid against him ought to have been warning enough. Though to give her credit, she'd never said another word about it after he'd proven the ridiculous story Ronnie had fed her wasn't true.

She seemed to believe what the judge and Ellamae had said about Ronnie's car accident.

But if he didn't watch his step around Kayla, if he didn't hold back on that overwhelming urge he'd been fighting to touch her, to do even more, he could find himself in trouble so deep, nothing anyone could say would get him out of it.

Chapter Twelve

Kayla sat beside the rolltop desk in Sam's office.

After their conversation, she had been relieved that he'd left the room. The attraction she felt for him only complicated an already intolerable situation.

Through the kitchen window a while later, she'd seen him go out to the barn. She had made a quick check on Becky, still out on the front porch with Sharleen, then had fled into the office for a much-needed break from the stress.

Now she held her fingers over the computer keyboard and began to type an instant message to Lianne, her fingers moving faster and faster as she went.

It's awful, Lianne. Just awful.

He's still insisting on hanging around you? Lianne typed back.

You bet he is.

Today had been the longest time they'd spent apart in weeks.

Beginning the day of her terrible accusation of him onward, he had spent every spare minute with her and

Becky, even escorting them into town several times to introduce them to more of his friends. She hadn't had the first opportunity to talk to any of these people without Sam close by. Even when she'd taken Becky to an art class earlier this week, he'd gone along.

Kayla hadn't taken an easy breath in days.

Constantly having him by her side only made her feel more mixed-up than ever.

Everyone seems to like me and accept me without question. She felt oddly grateful for that. Even Sharleen had come around, and they had slowly developed a polite but friendly relationship. What really gets to me is that they've all fallen in love with Becky.

And why not? Lianne shot back. She's adorable, smart and friendly. And not a bit shy. <grin>

LOL, Kayla replied, laughing.

Though Kayla was always on hand to interpret for her, Becky often got her point across without words when she needed to. Kayla couldn't help smiling at the child's resourcefulness.

If only the adults around her could manage even half as well. Or one adult, anyway.

When Kayla signed to Becky, she had begun to notice Sharleen watching. She'd even asked Kayla how to sign a few words.

Only Sam resisted.

Kayla knew she was partly to blame.

She still struggled to find answers to his challenge about deciding what she could believe. And to find a way to make up for her accusation. Even now, she didn't know what to think—or what to do.

And Sam… Sam didn't seem to want anything, except to prove his point with the judge.

The thought worried Kayla, filling her with panic and fear.

He's throwing his barbecue here, she typed, adding in all capital letters, THIS WEEKEND! And the judge is his guest of honor. What am I going to do?

You'll be fine. You'll figure something out. Have you heard anything from Matt yet?

No. To her dismay, Sam had turned up clean on the background check Matt had done. She had called him again just the day before, urging him to find something— anything—that would help her case for custody.

He'll come through for you. You know he will. Hang in there.

Kayla looked at the clock at the bottom of her screen. Her reprieve had ended. Time for dinner—and time to face Sam again.

Sighing, she said goodbye and closed the email program. Talking with Lianne about the day-to-day issues might help, but right now she didn't have the mental focus even to begin to explain her feelings about Sam. And what could she say, anyhow, when she couldn't understand them herself?

The recent weeks with Sam had only made things worse. And those moments of tension in the kitchen with him earlier had just about done her in.

They had also finally made her realize the truth.

She'd had an instant reaction to Sam. Oh, not five years ago. The stress and anger had been ratcheted too high for her to even think about him back then. And, of course, then he'd been married. But now that she'd come back to the ranch, there was no getting around her *current* interest in the man.

One look at him standing in the barn doorway the day she'd rushed here to get Becky had made her freeze in the front seat of her rental car. *One look.*

Broad shoulders and strong, sturdy hands, jet-black hair and glacier-gray eyes—any one of those things could do it for her every time. She'd never had the pleasure of seeing all those elements wrapped up in one neat package, though. The total effect was staggering.

She shouldn't let herself notice these things. Not about Becky's daddy. Not about Ronnie's ex. But she'd noticed now, and the feelings wouldn't go away. Worse, they turned traitor, twisting the situation around, filling her mind and heart with questions she couldn't begin to list in a message to Lianne.

Didn't want to think, even to herself.

What if she'd never come to Flagman's Folly that very first time? What if Sam hadn't had that bad memory of her to cling to? What if he didn't see her as the enemy, then and now?

But she had come, and he had seen her, and he would hold that against her forever. No sense in dreaming of what-ifs, of a past she couldn't change, a future she couldn't hope for.

Sighing, she swiveled her chair sideways, ready to get up from her seat. The front panel of the rolltop desk hadn't been closed completely. She saw something now she hadn't taken in before. On the surface of the desk, Sam had left a book. In the space between the desktop and the front panel, she could read enough of the title to know it was a dictionary. Not just any run-of-the mill dictionary. Not one that you'd find on the bookshelves of most homes.

A dictionary of American Sign Language.

Her heart squeezed painfully, for Becky or Sam or herself, she didn't know.

The sight of that book raised more questions she couldn't answer. Sharleen had gone in to Flagman's Folly only on the day of the parade, and she hadn't entered a store. Sam must have bought the dictionary. Why hadn't he mentioned it?

He wouldn't explain, of course. He already considered her nothing but a roadblock in his life. Well, she was about to get in his way a bit more.

That book proved Sam cared about finding a solution to the current situation so awkward for all of them. So heartbreaking for little Becky. The fact that he hadn't talked about the dictionary also proved he wasn't sure how to go about things.

Kayla did. If Sam couldn't reach out to her, she'd just have to reach out to him.

She would teach him to sign.

It would help them all in the short run, while they were still forced together by the judge. And in the long run…well, it would help then, too.

No matter how she tried not to, she had to acknowledge the truth. Becky needed her father in her life.

Even more reluctantly, she admitted Sam needed a place in Becky's life, too. When Kayla won custody—and she would—she couldn't be cruel enough to deny him visitation rights.

Beneath all these virtuous thoughts, she almost cringed at the ulterior motives racing through her mind.

Teaching Sam to sign might help make up for what she had done to him.

Teaching Sam to communicate with his daughter would show the judge how rational she was being about everything. How willing she would be to work with Sam to make sure he continued to have a place in Becky's life.

Just as long as that life was far away from this ranch. In Chicago. With Kayla.

WHAT WAS IT PEOPLE SAID about the best-laid plans?

A short while later, filled with confidence, Kayla sailed across the kitchen with the platter of pork roast and vegetables and anchored herself in her chair at the table. It took willpower for her to eat her dinner. To chat with Becky and Sharleen throughout the meal. To keep from blurting out her idea to Sam.

As she served the peach cobbler she had baked that morning, she made sure to set a generous slice in front of him.

Soon after, Sharleen went upstairs to her room. Becky, finished with the cookies she'd chosen over the cobbler, received permission to leave the table.

Alone with Sam at last, Kayla gripped her fork, cleared her throat and jumped into speech. "I'd like to teach you some sign, so you can talk to Becky. We're all going to be here together for a while longer, aren't we? We might as well put the time to good use."

He took the wind out of her sails with just one sentence. "That won't work."

"Of course it will." She forced a light laugh. "After all, I'm a certified sign language teacher." *I'll make it so easy for you, you'll see how uncomplicated it really is to talk with your daughter.*

"That's not what I meant. I don't have time to learn all that."

"Of course you do," she shot back. She'd started to sound like a talking doll whose recording had gotten stuck in the same groove. Taking a deep breath, she added slowly, "You have plenty of time. You've certainly proven that in the past few weeks."

He pushed his half-eaten dessert aside. "Judge's orders."

So, she *had* been right. He'd only spent his days with them so he could prove his own case in court. The knowledge made her even more determined to go through with her plan to upstage him.

Meanwhile, they still had the communication issue to deal with. For Becky's sake, she would give him one more chance to be reasonable. "I'll teach you in the evenings after Becky's gone to bed," she insisted. "You can certainly learn some of the most basic signs. We can make it a game for her." *And for you.*

"We've got enough games going on around here, don't you think?"

She blinked. "What does that mean? It seems like you're the one who's not playing straight with everything. I saw the sign language dictionary on your desk. Obviously, you've got some interest in learning to sign. Why don't you let me help you?"

"Thanks, but no thanks." Grabbing his dessert plate, he stood and walked over to the sink. "I've got it covered."

Not from anything she could see.

The man was impossible. He refused to do anything that would make it easier to communicate with his daughter. Why in the world did he even want custody of her? Just to prove another point—with his ex-wife?

She intended to find out, once and for all. Now. She slapped her palms on the table. Then she rose, turning to face him.

The sight of Becky standing in the doorway, a stuffed horse tucked under one arm and a wooly white lamb under the other, froze Kayla in place.

She smiled at her niece and could only hope the expression looked natural.

Sam had bought those animals the day of the parade in town, and Becky had kept them close ever since. Though it helped a little to know he cared, the toys didn't prove much. He could have bought the gifts to impress the people in town, just as he was planning that barbecue to influence the judge. Giving gifts wasn't the same as giving *himself,* something she'd never seen Sam do—and probably never would. Hadn't he admitted the time he grudgingly spent with Becky came directly by order of the judge? And he only suffered Kayla's presence because she refused to give up any chance to be with her niece.

What would happen in the awful event the judge awarded custody to Sam?

What kind of life would he provide for his daughter?

Through suddenly misty eyes, she looked at Becky again.

All the strategies Kayla had come up with to convince Sam to learn to sign seemed a waste of energy. The anger and contempt he felt for her didn't matter. The spark of attraction she felt for him and couldn't seem to put out permanently—though she'd smothered it often enough in frustration!—seemed trivial by comparison. Even the certainty that he'd felt a few sparks, too, did nothing for her now.

Everything seemed so unimportant compared to the child standing in front of them.

Her niece's well-being counted. It was all that mattered.

Even Sam Robertson, cold and inflexible as he was, would have to accept that.

As Becky ran back into the living room, Kayla took a half step toward Sam.

She found him staring through the kitchen doorway after his daughter. His frozen expression, the pain in his eyes, the shadow of something she couldn't name, all made her catch her breath. Fighting an overwhelming urge to reach out to him, she clenched her fingers and forced herself to keep her hands at her sides. Forced her feet to stay in place.

As if trying to hide his exposed emotions, he turned away. "Gotta go check on that mama cow in the barn," he muttered. A second later, the screen door slammed behind him as he left the house.

But he'd moved too late. She had already seen his reaction. The sight made her question her beliefs about him more than ever before.

She'd already fallen for one story Ronnie had told her, a story the judge and Ellamae had proved to be untrue. Maybe, instead of jumping to angry thoughts, she should give Sam the benefit of the doubt here.

The man was infuriating, though.

Was it only stubbornness on his part that made him refuse to learn to communicate with Becky? Only the limited time he had available, as he claimed? Or was there more behind his unwillingness to go along with Kayla's idea of teaching him sign language?

She thought again of his frozen expression as he'd

looked at his own child, of the shadow in his eyes, and her anger eased the slightest bit.

Could she already have seen the truth in his face?

Could Sam be afraid that he wouldn't learn to sign well enough to talk with Becky?

Chapter Thirteen

A little while after Kayla had tucked her niece into bed, Becky had appeared again in the living room. She'd argued against being brought back to her room but now, worn-out from playing with her dolls and stuffed animals, she had already fallen asleep.

Kayla resettled the toy horse and lamb beside her.

She left the room, her steps slow on the stairway down to the first floor as she planned her next move.

It was time to get serious with Sam.

She had made up her mind. She *would* make teaching him to sign into a game, and he'd learn the basics of the language whether he wanted to or not.

The challenge gave her no qualms at all.

Only the fact that this would put her even closer to him gave her second thoughts.

Downstairs, she found him half-sprawled on one of the couches. He watched her approach, his eyes heavy-lidded, looking on the verge of sleep himself.

Kayla couldn't take the couch opposite his, where Becky had so carefully arranged her family of dolls and the rest of her stuffed animals. Heart in her throat, she sat gingerly on the end of Sam's couch, as far from him as she could get.

Even as she took a breath, she admitted the lie to

herself. Of course, she could have moved the toys, could have sat facing him with the coffee table between them. But the thrill of knowing that one move of hers, one tiny slide across the cushions, would put her within touching distance of him had been a greater temptation than she could fight. With that one slide, Sam could pull her against him, could snuggle her close with his arm around her shoulders.

What would he feel when he held her? What would he think? More important, who would he see when he looked her way? Would he see her, Kayla, with her brown hair and blue eyes? Would he notice the tiny scar on her chin? Or would he focus only on her relationship to the ex-wife he so bitterly resented?

His eyes opened wider, and he shifted position on the couch. "Becky asleep?"

"Yes." She cleared her throat. "I made sure to stay with her until she drifted off."

"What brought her downstairs again?"

She shrugged. "A nightmare, probably." No surprise that she had picked up on the tension between the two adults during dinner. "I didn't question her. I was happy enough to have her fall back to sleep."

"No bedtime story tonight?"

"We read one after her bath."

"You've done that a lot." It was a statement, not a question.

"Yes, I have," she said, encouraged that he had mentioned it. "Ronnie leaves Becky at my mom and dad's often. I usually spend the night at my parents' house, too, whenever Becky's there. Although," she added, "they can communicate with her. They couldn't in the beginning. But my older sister and I taught them to sign." She looked at him. "You *could* learn, too, Sam."

He gave a gravelly laugh. "Nah. Can't teach an old dog new tricks."

So much for his assurance that he had things "covered." "My parents were older than you are now. And Sharleen seems to be picking up signs without any trouble."

"All right, then you can't force a young dog to learn new tricks."

Force. Was that what it would take for him to get the skills necessary to communicate with his daughter?

Then she recalled the expression she'd seen on his face when he'd looked at Becky.

The fear.

She had to come up with something to get him around that. But what? She thought for a moment then asked, "Have you ever donated blood?"

His brows rose. "Are you saying learning sign language is like giving blood?"

He gave a lopsided grin that had her heart rate soaring. But even that couldn't stop her. "I'm not kidding, Sam. Have you ever donated? Or even gone for bloodwork, maybe for an annual physical?"

"Well, yeah. Of course."

"What do they ask you to do to before they put the cuff on?"

He shrugged.

"Come on, I'm serious." She leaned across him to reach for his hand and lay it upright on the arm of the couch. She hadn't stopped to think things through, hadn't realized the move would bring their faces close. So close, their lips nearly touched. His breath tickled her cheek. His hand warmed her fingers. She'd been innocent in her sincerity, in her need to convince him to listen to her. But the gesture had backfired, stirring up additional emotions she didn't want to think about. She retreated to the safety of her corner of the couch.

"Show me," she said, wincing at the breathless sound of her voice.

Slowly, he curled his fingers into a fist, squeezed and released it a few times. "Like that?"

Though her lips trembled, she forced a smile. "Just like that. And with a slight change of palm orientation— the way you turn your hand—you've just made one of the most important signs Becky knows. One of the first she learned. The sign for *milk*."

He shook his head and looked away.

She held her breath, watching him. Whether he knew it or not, he was gently squeezing and opening the fingers of the fist he now rested on his knee.

She felt a sudden heaviness inside her chest. How could her heart harden into stone and break like glass, both at the same time?

"Give it a chance, Sam," she urged. She couldn't regret the pleading note in her voice. She was doing this for Becky.

"One word isn't going to get me very far." He stared off into the distance.

Again, she searched her mind for an argument that would prove otherwise. "What about that mama cow almost ready to give birth out in the barn? You said her calf would need a little time to get its legs under it, right?"

He refused to look her way.

She moved to stand in front of him, her hands on her hips to keep from reaching out. "You can't expect to match Becky's entire vocabulary in one easy lesson. And there *are* ways to communicate besides words, you know. You can learn those, too. Writing notes. Drawing pictures. Pointing. Gesturing. Even body language."

"Like this?" He rose from the couch and stepped forward to slide his arm around her waist, until she was braced against his chest. "And like this?" He tilted his head and looked down into her eyes. "And like this?" He matched his mouth to hers, kissing her with an intensity that sent a vibration all the way through her.

Kayla couldn't help herself. She'd dreamed of Sam's kiss for too many nights now. She'd seen that vulnerability in his face. That fear in his eyes. The man was human, after all. And too much temptation for her to resist. She couldn't just back off and walk away. Instead, she inched forward. He curled both arms around her, snuggling her close. He felt good against her, his hard planes a perfect balance for her curves, as if they'd been made to fit together.

She breathed deeply, taking in the scent of his aftershave mixed with the faint aroma of wood shavings, a surprising combination—but a lethally masculine one.

She couldn't stop herself from running her hands over his broad shoulders and up his tanned neck and, finally, tangling her fingers in his hair. When she gave a gentle tug, bringing his mouth closer yet, he inhaled raggedly and teased her lower lip with his teeth.

Suddenly, he backed away from her, leaving her hands in midair. Empty. She dropped her arms to her sides.

"Listen," he said, his voice rasping and deep, "it ought to be clear enough I'm never going to learn what it takes to talk to Becky. Why don't we quit all this playing around, and you just stay here with her? That'll solve all our problems at once."

"Stay here? You mean, permanently?" She choked on that last word.

"Yeah. You want to be with her. You can live with her here. Why not?"

"Why not?" she echoed.

He looked at her without speaking. She stared back, holding his gaze for what seemed a long time—long enough, anyhow, for her to see the gleam of some kind of emotion brighten his eyes.

Lust, probably.

She hoped her eyes didn't look the same. "I'll tell you *why not,* Sam." She moved out from behind the coffee table and past the end of the couch. Well beyond his reach. "I think you're out of your mind."

AFTER A LONG, RESTLESS night, Kayla walked down the stairs the next morning with Becky by her side. She'd made sure to wait until her niece had gathered up her toys and was ready to leave her bedroom. And she had her seated at the table long before Sam entered the kitchen. Not because she was afraid of him or of how he would react. Because she was worried about how *she* would react when she saw him.

When she'd left him last night, she had started away angry. The man was crazy. Certifiable, even.

By the time she'd gotten upstairs to her room, the full impact of his insulting words had sunk in. He'd expected her to jump at the chance to pick up her life in Chicago and move in with him—conveniently getting him off the hook for having to find another caretaker for Becky. Or worse, to learn to talk with her.

But it was only in the darkest hour of the night, as she tossed and turned, wide-awake, that the realization came to her. A realization she still didn't want to admit.

She had never in her life felt more hurt.

The door to the back porch opened. At the stove, Kayla stiffened, tightening her grip on the frying pan.

When Sam stepped into the room, Becky gave him a big grin. Kayla could have cried. Instead, she poured the eggs into the pan and turned on the teakettle.

"Breakfast will be ready shortly," she said.

"Yeah. I'd have been here sooner to help, but I just got done showering out in the bunkhouse. That calf decided to make her appearance last night."

"Everything went okay?"

She nearly shook her head at her own question. A few weeks ago, she couldn't have cared less—or known less—about the birthing of a calf.

A few short weeks ago, I hadn't cared so much about Sam.

Her quick inhalation turned into a gasp. She coughed, trying to cover it.

He reached toward her, as if to touch her elbow. When he saw her expression, he stopped, leaving his hand hovering in midair for a long moment before dropping it to his side. Just as she'd had to do the night before when he'd backed away from her.

"Yeah," he said, "everything went okay. The mama's fine. Baby, too. Already up on her feet, taking her first steps."

You could be, too, Sam.

He hesitated. "About last night. I'm sorry."

Her cheeks warmed, and she looked down at the frying pan, trying to concentrate on breakfast. She didn't want to think about last night. About Sam's body against hers in that tight space between the couch and the coffee table. About that insane suggestion he had made.

She looked across the kitchen. Despite how uncomfortable Kayla felt with Sam beside her, she couldn't help smiling at her niece. Becky had her head down, her eyes intent on her drawing pad. Matt's wife, Kerry, the art teacher, said Becky had the determination and drive to become a good artist someday.

The reminder of the lawyer made the smile slide from Kayla's lips. She should be on the phone with him now, not standing here waffling over how to respond to Sam. Before she could figure out what to say, he spoke again.

He ran his hand along the edge of the counter, not looking at her. "Wasn't thinking last night, I guess. Or, more likely, I was thinking—and doing—all the wrong things."

She scraped the spatula across the pan, stirring the eggs. They looked about as scrambled as her emotions right then. But she wouldn't let him see how much his crazy idea had hurt her. "I suppose I should apologize, too," she said, forcing a cool tone. "I guess we were both doing the wrong things."

Still, she couldn't bring herself to look his way.

This time, when she glanced over toward Becky, she managed to catch her niece's eye. She lifted her hand to her mouth, fingers cupped, then gestured with that same hand held palm up. *"What do you want to drink?"*

Becky squeezed her fingers into a fist, and Kayla's heart suddenly felt as if it had been squeezed tightly, too.

"Milk."

The sign she had shown Sam the night before.

Before she could move, he opened the refrigerator door and reached in. When he pulled his hand out, he was holding a plastic gallon-size jug. She stared at him. He met her eyes and froze in place.

Her heart seemed to tighten again, and for a long moment, she struggled to blink back tears.

The man might be nuts.

But maybe…just maybe…there was hope for him yet.

"It's all right," she said softly, unable to ignore the stunned look in his eyes. "Just like that baby calf of yours, you've taken your first step."

Chapter Fourteen

Sam got through breakfast. Somehow. He felt like he'd eaten in his sleep, and not only from getting up so early for the birth of the calf.

Kayla was quiet all through the meal, too.

Neither of them responded much to Sharleen's attempts at conversation. Finally, she gave up, saying she and Becky would be out on the front porch. But as they left the room, she glanced back over her shoulder. Sharleen knew something was up between the other two adults.

He knew exactly what was bothering Kayla. She had nailed it the night before. He was out of his mind, all right, or else he'd never have blurted out that dumb suggestion. Crazy as a loon, for sure—over Kayla Ward.

The thought almost made him drop the glass he'd been loading into the dishwasher.

If that kiss they had shared…that kiss *he* had started wasn't enough to tell him the woman was trouble, the reminder of her last name definitely shouted it loud and clear. He needed to get away from her.

"I'm going out to check on that calf."

She just nodded.

But when he left the kitchen and went down the back porch steps, he heard the door open and close again behind him. He stopped in his tracks. He couldn't talk to her right now. He felt too churned up. Too raw. Things were happening he wasn't prepared for, and he hadn't the first clue what to do about them.

But he'd already made a mess of the situation. Ignoring her would only make everything worse.

Slowly, he turned back.

To his surprise, he found Kayla had not followed him out onto the porch, after all. Becky had. She stood on the top step, looking up at him with those silver-gray eyes so like his own.

He stood frozen, just as he had done when he realized he had understood her request for the milk.

He'd understood her.

Kayla was right. It *was* a first step in building a relationship with his baby. And now he was being offered another one. If he wanted it.

If he could get up the courage to go for it.

He'd missed so many opportunities to be with his daughter. Been denied so many chances to spend time with her. How could he let another one slip by?

"Hey, Becky," he said softly, "want to go look at a brand-new calf with me?"

He knew she couldn't hear him. Couldn't understand. Would she take him on trust, anyway?

Barely able to breathe, he held out his hand to her.

For a second, his entire body trembled. A very real tremor that shook him down to his boots as he waited to see how his daughter would react.

In another second, he knew.

She looked up, her eyes sparkling in the morning sunshine, her face so innocent. And she put her hand in his.

His eyes blurred. He blinked again and again, but no

matter how many times he tried, he couldn't seem to make them clear. With his free hand, he rubbed both eyelids, hard.

Becky came down the steps, her fingers still wrapped securely around his.

Shortening his stride to match hers, he led her across the yard and over toward the barn. He'd show her the new calf and its mama. Bring her out back of the barn to see the chickens. Take her for a ride on the calmest horse in his stable.

All of a sudden, he had a whole list of things he wanted to show Becky.

He had a lot of lost time to make up for.

KAYLA STOOD AT THE SINK, looking through the kitchen window and feeling the need to wring her hands like the heroine of an old silent movie. Some heroine she was.

Sharleen had gone up to her room after Becky had left with Sam. It had been more than an hour since then, and it was taking all Kayla's willpower not to go track them down.

Becky could handle herself with Sam, that much she knew.

Reverse the roles, and she wouldn't place any bets on Sam. He'd been so resistant to learning to sign.

She had watched through this window earlier, when he had left the kitchen and Becky had followed. When he had reached out and his daughter had put her small hand into his.

His daughter.

Kayla gripped the edge of the sink, trying to anchor herself. Trying to stop the thoughts that were whirling in her head.

The fear that she could lose Becky. The knowledge

that she was weakening when it came to Sam. She couldn't lose. And she couldn't weaken, couldn't give in. Any indication of backing down, and he'd be all over that like ice cream on a summer sidewalk.

Through the window, she suddenly saw him emerge from the wide doorway of the barn. Alone. But as she watched, she discovered he held a horse's reins. As he walked slowly forward, she saw the horse appear, too.

With Becky sitting upright in the saddle.

Kayla's heart seemed to leap to her throat. She rushed across to the back door and out onto the porch.

"Sam," she hissed, afraid that yelling his name might startle the horse.

He looked her way, put up a hand to stop the animal and waited while she crossed the yard toward them.

"What are you doing?" she asked.

He shrugged. "What it looks like. Taking Becky for a ride."

"On a huge horse like that? She's too little to be up on him all by herself."

"No, she's not. Heck, kids around here start to ride practically before they start to walk."

"Well, she's not from around here and she's not used to horses."

"*I* am."

She wanted to wipe the smirk from his face. "That horse is three times as tall as Becky." At least, it looked that way.

He laughed. "Don't worry about it. The mare's a cream puff. I'll give you a ride on her next, if you want."

She scowled at him. "That offer's about as funny as the last one you made to me. Will you please take Becky down?"

"Why? She's having a great time."

Becky did look happy, way up there on the horse's back. That didn't make Kayla feel any better. For all her insistence over the years that her niece needed to be independent, that the child could handle herself, there were some situations she just could not manage. Kayla felt sure this was one of them. Though you couldn't tell it by the grin on Becky's face.

"Sam."

Instead of doing as she had asked and taking Becky down from the horse, he put his foot in the stirrup and hoisted himself up, settling in the saddle behind her.

"There. Now she's not all by herself." He did something with the reins that made the animal turn and start walking away. He looked at Kayla over his shoulder. "We'll be fine," he assured her.

"Sam," she said from between gritted teeth.

Another flick of the reins, and the horse started off at a trot. Becky gave her an excited wave goodbye.

Clutching her hands together, Kayla watched them go. She wasn't overreacting. She wasn't.

But in her heart, she knew she was. Not to the fact that Becky was up on the horse, but that Sam had ignored her request. Had taken her niece away from her, despite the protest she'd made.

Was this an omen of what was to come?

The thought turned her hands to ice. She could barely open the screen door. Once she'd grabbed her cell phone from the kitchen counter, she had to fumble to punch the buttons.

"Answer, answer," she muttered when the ringing began at the other end. To her relief, a moment later, she heard Matt's voice on the line.

"Matt," she said, gulping, trying desperately to calm

herself so he wouldn't know how agitated she was. "Just checking in. I wanted to see if you'd found out anything yet about Sam."

"Yes, as a matter of fact, I was planning to call shortly. I finally got some info on that suggestion you had about an incident when he was a teenager."

"You did?" She gripped the cell phone more tightly. At last, she was going to find out something that would give her custody of Becky once and for all. "And—?"

"And it turns out, he'd almost done jail time when he was seventeen. He set fire—accidentally, he claims—to a barn on a neighboring property."

She gasped. "No one was hurt?" Despite the news and what it might do to help her cause, she couldn't stop herself from asking the question. The thought of Ronnie's accusation ran through her mind. She pushed it away, hard. The judge and Ellamae had shown her that wasn't true. She trusted Sam.

Yet, he had just gone off, alone, who knew where, with Becky.

She shook her head. Everything was all right.

"No one was hurt," Matt confirmed.

She gave a sigh of relief.

"But it's still not good, Kayla. Half the livestock inside the barn died from the smoke. The barn was considered a complete loss. And the family had no insurance to cover any of it. From what we were able to gather, Robertson's mother made restitution for her son, but the Porter family holds a grudge against him to this day."

Kayla closed her eyes against a sudden painful stinging beneath her lids. How awful for that to happen. And how terrible for Sam to have to live with it. It had to have been an accident. She refused to believe he could do something like that on purpose. Not Sam, who lived on a ranch filled with animals.

Now she could even understand his reluctance to have Pirate on his property. The dog belonged to that family next door.

Refusing to believe in Sam's guilt only increased her own. She knew she would use this information against him if she could.

She had to.

"What happened after?" she asked Matt.

"He got off lucky. He was sentenced to a substantial number of hours of community service and had to report in to the local judge weekly for quite some time."

"The *local* judge? What was his name?"

"Hang on, let me check." She heard computer keys clicking in the background, but already her spirits were sinking. "Here it is. The Honorable Lloyd M.—"

"Baylor," she finished in the same breath. She sighed. "I'm afraid that's a dead end. He's the same judge we're dealing with now. He already knows about what happened back then. The information won't do us any good."

"True," he agreed.

"So we're no further along than we were before." She dropped into the nearest chair at the kitchen table. "And time's running out, Matt. I'm getting desperate. The judge is due here this Sunday for a good old-fashioned barbecue—and I just know Sam plans to pull out all the stops to win him over to his side."

"I haven't given up," Matt said.

"I know, but it's only two days away—"

"We'll keep digging. Just hold tight."

A noise sounded in the yard. She raised her head and

caught her breath. Through the window, she heard the sound of a horse's whinny.

Sam had come back with Becky.

She stood and moved over to the back door, keeping to the side so he wouldn't see her. In one fluid movement, he swung himself from the horse's back to the ground. When he reached up, Becky stretched both hands out to him. He lifted her from the saddle and set her beside him.

Even from this distance, Kayla could see her niece's flushed face and sparkling eyes. Could see Sam's grin as he stroked Becky's hair.

Kayla's grip on the phone made her knuckles hurt. "Yes, keep digging, Matt," she said. She had to force the words past her tight throat. "Do what you can. And, please, do it fast."

Chapter Fifteen

Early the next morning, Kayla stood beside Sam at the cash register at Harley's General Store as he paid the bill. She ran her hands up and down her arms, trying to warm them. They'd spent too much time in the frozen food aisle while Becky deliberated over the ice cream. If Sam had gotten his way, Kayla didn't doubt, he would have bought every flavor in the freezer case.

"I need to thaw out," she told him, reaching for the handle of their overflowing cart. Sam had told her all the food for the barbecue would be taken care of, but she and Sharleen between them had come up with a long list of things they still needed. "Becky and I will take the groceries to the truck."

"All right."

She gestured for Becky to leave the store ahead of her.

Outside, Kayla hurried over to Sam's pickup truck and transferred everything into the flatbed, making sure to load the three gallons of ice cream Sam had insisted on buying into the insulated cooler they'd brought. Good thing she had remembered the cooler, or they would have left a trail of sweet ooze all the way back to the ranch.

Becky, standing beside her, suddenly gave her happy

screech. One hand clapped over her eye, she took off across the sidewalk.

Pirate.

Here in town?

Kayla turned. The puppy was indeed here. He sprawled, belly flat, on the cement walk outside the barbershop. When he saw Becky running toward him, the puppy bounded to his feet. He lunged forward but was stopped short by the leash around his neck. The other end of the leash seemed to be tied tightly to a railing outside the shop.

The leather strap gave him enough leeway to jump, though, and he leaped back and forth, tail wagging, until Becky reached him.

She patted his head. Then she grabbed at his tail with one hand, pushed at his rump with the other, somehow managing to get him to sit still. But not for long. He rolled over onto his back, exposing his underside for a belly rub.

Kayla laughed. He was such a cute pup. So patient with Becky, too. And she seemed to have no fear of him at all.

After the rub, Becky reached for the leash, tugging on it as if trying to pull it loose from the railing.

Kayla started forward. She had made it halfway to the barbershop when a stocky, red-faced man burst through the doorway. With his hair half-combed, he looked as if he'd jumped out of his chair before Lou, the barber, had finished his job.

"Hey, you," the man called, "leave that leash alone. Hey! Did you hear what I said? Drop it." He tried to pry Becky's fingers from the strap.

She gave a startled, high-pitched cry.

"Wait a minute," Kayla called, doubling her speed. "*You* leave *her* alone. She can't hear you!"

"*Porter!*"

The roar came from behind Kayla, drowning out her final words. Before she could turn, someone brushed by her, nearly knocking her off balance.

Sam.

He put his hand on the man's elbow. "Take your mitts off my kid."

"Or what?" Porter demanded, shouldering Sam aside.

The shove pushed Sam into Pirate, who had sprung up and begun jumping back and forth again. In turn, Sam's weight pushed the dog against Becky, who lost her footing and fell against the rail.

Sam swung at the other man. The sight of his fist connecting with Porter's chin made Kayla wince.

A crowd had started to gather, drawn from the barbershop and Harley's.

She rushed over to the two men and wedged herself between them.

"Sam." She put her hand on his arm. "Let's go, okay?"

He stared past her at his neighbor. "Not okay."

Porter backed off, rubbing his jaw and glaring at them.

"We don't want a scene," she hissed, nearly into Sam's ear. "And you especially don't want one with this man."

For a long moment, he did nothing. Then he silently took Becky by the hand and walked away.

As Kayla breathed a sigh of relief, Becky gave one last look over her shoulder and waved goodbye to Pirate.

Porter yanked on the leash. The pup let out a low growl.

"Everything's fine, folks," Sam called.

"That's good to hear." Lou had been hovering in the doorway of his shop. After nodding at Kayla, the barber stepped back and closed the door in Porter's face.

She hurried to catch up to Sam. He had already settled Becky in her booster seat in the truck. Kayla climbed into the cab and had barely strapped herself in when he started the engine. He took off with a burst of speed that bounced her back against the seat.

She looked over her shoulder. Becky sat looking out the window at Pirate.

"Sam," Kayla said, "it would be nice to get home with the groceries still in the truck."

"Yeah." He growled the word. And sounded almost exactly like Pirate. But the truck slowed.

"What is it with you and Porter?" she demanded.

"You seemed to know all about it, with that warning you gave me."

She shook her head. "Not all. Just some."

"Where do you get your information?"

She hesitated.

"Don't bother," he added. "I can guess. The women of Flagman's Folly are always ready for a good gossip."

Feeling her cheeks flush, she adjusted the air conditioner vent. Finally, she said, "I'd rather hear the full story from you. The true one."

A long pause, as he drove slowly down Signal Street and along the back lanes already familiar to her, that took them out of town.

She should have known he wouldn't answer her.

But when he turned, at last, onto the road that led to the ranch, he surprised her.

"How much do you know already?" he asked.

"Well." She chose her words carefully from Matt's

report. "When you were a teenager, there was an accident, a fire on the Porters' property. And there were animals lost."

"Kind of cold, isn't it?"

She frowned, puzzled.

"Say it like it was, Kayla."

"You mean…"

"No, *you* mean, I started a fire in the Porters' barn, and I killed off half the livestock in it."

"You forgot the accident part."

"Who said it was an accident?"

She turned abruptly toward him and almost choked when the seat belt stopped short. Now she knew how poor Pirate had felt with that leash around his neck. She loosened the strap. "Come on, Sam. I know you wouldn't do something like that on purpose."

She believed him.

The knowledge rocked him, making Sam grip the steering wheel so hard, he thought he'd leave permanent grooves. A mile down the road later, he still couldn't get over it.

Or figure out how to answer her.

Kayla believed him, but she didn't understand how much she was asking of him by wanting to know the full story. There were details about that night in the Porters' barn that no one else had ever learned.

No one could learn them, because he'd made a promise to the only other person who knew what had happened. A teenage promise that had gone a long way toward helping screw up his life.

But Kayla sat there looking at him, waiting for him to answer.

Trusting him, for once, to tell her the truth.

He shifted his grip on the wheel, looked at the road ahead and in his rearview mirror. No one else in sight. They might have been alone, the three of them.

Except for the man he'd never forgotten, who could just as well be riding alongside him now, invisible, for all that Sam couldn't force him from his mind.

And except for the animals who'd been trapped in the burning building. The memory of them stayed with him, too.

"We'd gone into the barn that night to get out of the cold," he said slowly.

"You and...?"

"Porter."

"The man who owns Pirate?"

He nodded.

"He'd turned on a kerosene lamp, low. We could just about see our hands in front of our faces. Enough to do what we wanted to do." He flexed his fingers, then tightened them on the wheel again. "We had a bottle of whiskey he'd taken from his old man's stash in the garage. First time we'd ever done that. Felt like a real kick to be sneaking into the barn, hanging out like the ranch hands did." He paused, then went on. "We both got stupid-drunk."

He glanced at his mirrors again then looked in his rearview at Becky. She was turning the pages of a picture book.

Kayla sat watching him intently.

He shrugged. "We started goofing around with the hay and next thing we knew, we had started a fire we couldn't control."

She sucked in a breath so loud, he could hear it over the hum of the pickup's tires against the road. "You didn't do it deliberately."

"No, but we were under the influence. And it was my fault."

"Yours? How can you say that? It sounds like you both messed up."

"Yeah, but I was the one who'd come up with the idea of taking the whiskey."

She said nothing. She didn't need to. He knew what she was thinking. *So much for trusting him now. So much for asking him for the truth.* He'd never lied before the night of that fire. A couple days later, after leaving the courtroom, he'd sworn he'd never do so again. But that one lie of omission in front of the judge had hurt him ever since.

Finally, she spoke. "What happened? With the fire?"

He stared, unblinking, into the distance, trying to get the words from his throat. "Some of the rags the ranch hands used to polish the tack started smoldering, too. We barely had time to blink before we were surrounded by smoke and flames. We...we headed for the animals. Tried to get them out of their stalls. They were scared. Confused. In a panic. So were we."

The road ahead was clear.

He couldn't help himself, he had to close his eyes for the briefest of moments. Had to try to shut out the sights from that night. The sounds, the smell.

A second later, his eyes shot open again. The blackness behind his lids only made the images more clear, the memories more real, like watching a movie projected on a screen in a darkened theater. Cold sweat ran down his brow.

"You can't repeat any of this, Kayla. No one knows Porter was there that night."

"*What?* How could they not know?" He could hear the bewilderment in her tone.

"The ranch hands were there in no time, but every-thing was in chaos. Later, Porter said he'd been in the house and run out to do what he could to help."

"Sam…" She shook her head. "I just don't under-stand. Why would you let him get away with that? Why would you take all the blame, when he was right there with you?"

"He begged me to. He'd been in trouble so often his old man had threatened the next time he would ship him off to military school."

"Maybe that's what he needed."

"Maybe. Who knows now?" He sighed. "But back then, it was a big deal, and he was scared as hell his old man would follow through. Back then, we were best friends. He begged me to cover for him, and I did. And you can't repeat *any* of this," he said again. "I gave him my solemn promise no one would ever know. And even seeing the kind of scum he's turned out to be, I won't go back on my word."

KAYLA LOOKED AT THE MANTEL clock. Not yet time for her to start lunch—or dinner, as they called the noon meal here. She sank onto one of the living-room couches with a cushion cradled in her arms.

On the opposite couch, Sam sat with a ledger spread open across his lap and a calculator balanced on one knee. He'd been at it since they'd come home that af-ternoon, figuring and crumpling up scrap paper and figuring again. Becky knelt on the floor, her coloring book and crayons taking up most of the space on the coffee table.

The two of them wore nearly identical frowns of concentration.

Kayla held back a groan and hugged the pillow more tightly to her.

After the fight between Sam and his neighbor, she had been frantic to get Sam out of there before any more damage was done. She couldn't blame him for his reaction. She might have done the same herself. Wasn't she already rushing to Becky's aid when he had gone running past?

And that creep, Porter, had been manhandling a four-year-old!

Kayla didn't know which to be more thankful for, the fact that Sam had stood up for Becky, or that he had trusted her with the truth about his next-door neighbor and their past.

Hearing the story about the fire had shown her Sam in a different light, too. Yes, he had done a stupid thing. But he'd paid the price for it, probably in more ways than one. She could see that in his face when he'd talked about the loss of the animals in the barn.

How could she hold either of those episodes against him?

For all those years, he had honored a promise he'd made to a friend—although to a friend who didn't deserve Sam's loyalty.

And today, at least he'd been fighting for his daughter, instead of ignoring her as he had done for so long. Nothing else would have even come close to affecting her. But the show of support for Becky forced Kayla to admit the truth.

Both from her own observations lately and from the certainty that had taken root in her, she knew Sam *wanted* to be a good daddy to his daughter. He just didn't know how.

Across from her, he tossed a crumpled-up sheet of

paper onto the coffee table. Becky laughed and batted it back toward him.

He smiled. The wistfulness of his expression tore at Kayla's heart.

Becky got to her feet and ran off to the kitchen, where she'd left her dolls.

Kayla looked back at Sam and forced herself to keep her voice steady, her words light. "Having troubles?" she asked, glancing at the wads of paper all around him.

"Yeah. Color problems. Trying to turn red into black."

Before she could ask what he meant, he leaned forward and picked up one of Becky's crayons. With a grin, he held his hand out to her, the crayon balanced on his open palm. "How do you say *black* in sign?"

Kayla drew an invisible line across her forehead with the tip of her index finger. "What did you mean, you're 'trying—?'"

"How about *red?*" He picked up another crayon. "How do you sign that?" He seemed to want to distract her from what he had said.

Slowly, she touched her same index finger below her mouth and brushed the tip downward and off her chin. His gaze lingered on her bottom lip.

He rose from his couch and came around the coffee table to sit beside her.

She clutched the cushion she had dropped into her lap.

"Green?" he asked, grabbing another crayon.

She held her thumb and index finger a half inch apart. Luckily, she needed to shake her hand to form the sign for *green,* because her fingers were already trembling.

"Blue?" he asked, looking directly at her.

She glanced down at his empty hand. "N-no fair. You're not holding a blue crayon."

"I was talking about your eyes. They're blue. Very blue. And your cheeks are bright pink all of a sudden." He smiled and leaned closer. "I can learn *all* my colors," he murmured, "just by looking at you."

Her heart thumped heavily. She wanted to lean back but couldn't. She should get up and walk away. Somehow, she couldn't do that, either. "There are more signs than just colors, you know." Her voice cracked on the last word.

He smiled. He knew just what he was doing to her. And darn him, he was enjoying it.

"True." He nodded. "How do you say *I?*"

She pointed her index finger at herself.

"And how do you say *want?*"

"You…do this." She held both palms up and crooked all her fingers as she pulled her hands toward her body.

He leaned even closer. "And how do you say *a kiss?*" he whispered.

"Uhh…" She paused. "I forget." She had to draw the line somewhere.

Didn't she?

Chuckling, he shook his head. "Well, maybe this will help your memory." He slid his arm around her waist and held her close.

Before she could react, could close her eyes or even take a breath, Becky's high-pitched laughter rang out. She stood in the kitchen archway, her shoulders hiked up near her ears and her hands trying to cover the huge grin splitting her face.

A gesture that could probably be understood in any language.

Then she put the fingertips of each hand together and pursed her lips.

"Saved," Kayla said, gently pushing Sam away. "You've just seen the sign for *kiss*."

Chapter Sixteen

Sam slid the lengths of pine onto his workbench and flipped the switch to turn off the saw. As usual on a Saturday night, Jack and the boys had gone into town and he had the workshop in one corner of the bunkhouse to himself.

Or maybe not.

As the whine of the saw faded, footsteps tapped against the hallway floor. Kayla stepped through the doorway. He tightened his grip on the plank.

"Becky's almost ready for bed, and she was wondering where you were." Her smile seemed strained.

"Looks like you found me," he said. Great answer. Tongue-tied and awkward as he'd suddenly felt, he couldn't come up with anything better. Teasing her on the couch in the living room had been one thing.

Seeing her here in his workshop, the place he went to when he needed to escape, was something else.

"I followed the noise of the saw," she said.

He nodded. Something Becky wouldn't have been able to do. The thought hurt. "I'll come over to the house in just a few minutes."

"Okay." She looked around the shop, seeming to take everything in. Her gaze lingered on his latest piece, a stallion he'd stained in a shade so dark it gleamed like onyx in the fluorescent light over the workbench. "This is beautiful," she said quietly.

He shrugged.

"They're *all* beautiful." She indicated the plaques and carvings and inlaid pieces on the shelves lining the room. "All horses. And every one of them is running, like the horse on Becky's headboard."

"They're free," he muttered.

"And they're alive?" she asked softly.

He dug his nails into the wood he still held. How had she caught on to that?

"Sam, what happened after the fire? To you, I mean."

Carefully, he set the plank down on his workbench. He'd told her more than he should have this afternoon. Did he want to satisfy her question now? If he refused, would he discover she'd already found out the answer to that, too?

Better to tell her himself than to have her tell *him* whatever rumors she'd heard.

"After the fire, I went crazy," he said bluntly. "My daddy had died and my mother was grieving and she was in no shape to ride herd on me. The judge tried. Gave me community service. But once I'd served the time, I started drinking, hanging out at the bar. Then I got bored and moved around some. That's when I met Ronnie. Abilene, at a rodeo—as I might have told you. As I also might have said," he added dryly, "that's when I found myself hitched. It was a wild time and a wild ride, and I was a no-account fool."

"Maybe."

"Definitely. It took me a while, but I finally settled down again."

"Don't you think you might have been grieving, too? For your father and—" she indicated the wooden carvings on the shelves around them "—for what happened that night in the barn?"

Without answering, he turned back to his workbench.

She waited awhile, then finally walked out.

He should have been glad she'd left him alone here in the only place he ever truly felt at peace. Yet at the sound of the workshop door closing, he had to stop himself from going after her. Where was his pride now?

He might have settled down again, but it seemed he'd gone right back to acting like a no-account fool.

SUNDAY MORNING. A PERFECT DAY for a barbecue.

Kayla wasn't sure how she felt about that.

Though the heat still hovered near the hundred mark, the recent wave of high humidity had broken. Once in a while, a cloud took it upon itself to scoot in front of the sun. She appreciated the occasional shady moments, but she had still made sure to slather herself and Becky with sunscreen over every exposed patch of skin.

She could have used something to protect the inside of her body, too. Namely, her heart. Sam's story last night had just about broken it in two.

Thankfully, she had enough to do in the kitchen to keep her busy. If only the jobs could keep her far enough from the kitchen window to avoid her frequent sights of Sam. Out in the yard, he worked as hard as his cowboys did, setting up trestles and boards for tables, getting pits and spits and things she'd never heard of ready for the barbecue.

"Well," Sharleen said, distracting her, "that's it on the sweet tea and lemonade. We've made enough to fill a bathtub apiece."

"Very true. Paper towels and utensils are done, too."

She'd layered them into the wicker baskets now ready on the kitchen table. Serving trays filled with condiments lined the counter. "I think we've crossed everything off the list."

"Not a minute too soon, either." Sharleen sighed. With the doctor's okay, she had stopped using the crutches, but Kayla noticed she seemed in more pain without them.

"Let's go outside," she urged the older woman. "You can put your feet up, and we can see how things are going."

She tapped the tabletop to get Becky's attention, and the three of them moved out to the front porch.

Her niece reached between two slats of the porch railing and waved energetically at Sam and Jack, who now stood in conference near the barn. When Sam motioned for Becky to join them, she nearly flew across the yard.

Watching her, Kayla shook her head. "Those sneakers," she said ruefully. Last night, Becky had decided to decorate her brand-new white sneakers, taking a purple marker and covering the pristine canvas with bright stars. "Well, at least she used a washable marker."

Sharleen laughed. "Chances are, grass stains will cause more problems than the stars."

Becky had reached Sam, who patted the top of the fence and made the sign Kayla had shown him for *want.*

Becky nodded eagerly, and he lifted her up to sit on the railing.

Again, Kayla shook her head.

Can't teach an old dog new tricks, Sam had said not so long ago. Now that he had given in, finally, about learning to talk to Becky, it turned out he had no trouble at all picking up the basic signs Kayla had taught him the night before. He'd even admitted how much easier he found it to learn from her, rather than trying to understand the dictionary he had bought. She also suspected that, for days now, he'd been paying closer attention to her signs at the dinner table than she had realized.

Everything seemed to be falling into place for him.

The thought was bittersweet.

"I'm going to start putting the trays out," she told Sharleen.

Now that she'd succeeded in getting the other woman comfortable and off her feet, she needed to go back to work. She had made sure to get up early that morning to do her share. Not one person from Flagman's Folly would be able to call her a slacker!

She had just returned to the kitchen when she heard the front door close again. She moved through the archway into the living room to investigate. Sam knelt in front of the entertainment center, pulling boxes from its lower section.

"You could have told me you needed something from the house," she said, crossing the room. "I'd have been happy to get it."

"No problem."

She looked down at the boxes. Checkers and chess and other games for the kids to play with. "If I'd known you'd had these," she said, "we could have been playing them all along with Becky."

"We still can." He rose, his arms filled with boxes, and pretended to leer at her. "And we can try some other games once she goes to bed." Laughing, he walked to the front door.

She followed, frowning.

By the time she reached the porch, he was already disappearing around the corner of the house.

Along the road from town, a procession of pickup trucks and cars approached the ranch. The residents of Flagman's Folly were about to arrive. Suddenly, her throat felt dry and her hands damp.

As she had told Lianne, everyone she'd met seemed to like her. Everyone but Judge Baylor, the one person who held her fate in his hands. One of these vehicles could be bringing him here. Bringing him closer to a decision.

The judge's imminent arrival had twisted her nerves tighter by the hour.

Sam's attentions only made everything worse.

No matter how much he joked with her, no matter how many signs he was willing to learn, she couldn't let him get to her. Theirs was a temporary relationship. She couldn't forget her permanent goal.

One of the pickup trucks pulled to a stop at the side of the road. The others lined up behind. Children seemed to spill from every vehicle. Seconds later, the yard filled with people and chatter and the smell of good food.

She glanced over toward Becky, who now stood leaning against the fence. When she caught Kayla looking her way, she hooked her index fingers together briefly, then quickly reversed the hand position several times.

"Friends."

Nodding, Kayla bobbed her fist in the air and fought back tears. For Becky, there wouldn't be any undercurrents, any history behind her conversations today. Becky, at least, would have a fun, carefree time playing with the children she'd taken the class with at the arts center and with others she would meet this afternoon. And Lianne had called it right—their niece certainly wasn't shy.

Kayla was no pushover, either. She straightened her shoulders, uncurled her clenched fingers, and smiled at the women coming toward her, their hands filled with carrying bags and casserole dishes.

"Good to see you, ladies," she said brightly. "We've got tables set up in the backyard."

As she ushered them past the house, she glanced at the people still streaming from the long line of vehicles at the side of the road. No sign of the judge so far. Maybe something had come up, and he wouldn't be able to attend the barbecue today.

Could she be that lucky?

NO SUCH LUCK.

By the time late afternoon rolled around, the judge had not only made his entrance, he had become the hub around which the entire barbecue revolved.

Kayla should have known.

Worse, when the last sticky hand and face had been wiped with the oversize paper towels they'd used as napkins, the last ear of corn had been chewed to the nub, and the last dessert crumb had disappeared, the judge leaned back in his chair—one brought especially for him from the front porch—and grinned a barbecue-eating grin.

"Good stuff, huh, Judge?" Sam said.

She could have kicked him under the makeshift tabletop.

"Right tasty," the man agreed. He turned to Dori, seated beside him. "That caramel custard thing was just about this side of pure bliss."

She smiled.

Manny, on her other side, leaned forward. "She makes magic with pastry, my Dori."

"That she does."

"What do you say, Judge?" Sam asked. "You up for a round of horseshoes?"

"Sam," Kayla said sweetly, "we've just finished eating."

"Yeah. No problem."

"I think it might be." She widened her eyes, all innocence. "Don't you think Judge Baylor might want some time to relax?"

"Relax?" The judge sat up. "Who needs time for relaxing? What are you trying to pull here, young lady?" He laughed, but the laserlike gaze he shot her way made her shiver. "I've got to burn off some of this food and get myself ready for seconds on those sweets."

Beside her, Sam smiled. He held his index and middle fingers in the shape of a *V*, palm inward, near his eye. *"See?"*

She gritted her teeth and ground her heels into the dirt beneath the table. Yes, he'd turned into a quick study. And at the moment, a huge annoyance.

It wasn't the horseshoe game that bothered her. And she didn't want to turn Judge Baylor against Sam. She just wanted the man here, where he could see her interacting with Becky. Not over at the other end of the yard bonding with her niece's father.

"Let's go, young Robertson," the judge said. "And anyone else fool enough to think they can take me on."

Sam stayed long enough to turn to Kayla. "Keep an eye on Becky, okay?"

"Nothing to worry about," she assured him. "She'll be fine."

Following in the wake of every adult male in sight,

he made a beeline down the length of the yard to the spot he had designated for the horseshoe toss.

"Well." Frowning, she stared after them. "Not one of them seemed to have a problem figuring out where to go."

"They know already," Dori assured her. "Every year, Sam sets the horseshoes there."

"Yeah," Ellamae said with a laugh. "As far as they can all get from the kitchen and still seem sociable."

Kayla frowned again. Good thing she'd applied fresh sunscreen, or by tonight, she'd have red-and-white stripes from sunburn on her forehead. "You mean the women do all the cleaning up? That doesn't seem fair."

"Oh, we plan it that way," Sharleen told her, "else we wouldn't have a chance."

"A chance…?"

"At Dori's desserts," Ellamae explained. "We get first crack at the next round of 'em."

"Oh." Kayla smiled. "Well, that's not such a bad idea, after all. I wonder how the judge will feel about it?"

"What he doesn't know can't hurt him," Ellamae said with a wink.

"And," Dori added, "we have the time to share gossip."

"Even better," Kayla said, crossing her fingers beneath the table. "Who's going first?"

But by the time the dishes were out of the way and the second round of desserts begun, she'd learned nothing of interest to her. While the news of who'd been caught substituting commercial jam for homemade at the last county fair had horrified the women of Flagman's Folly, it didn't do much for Kayla's curiosity about Sam.

On the way home from town yesterday and in his workshop last night, he had shared more than she had dared hope about his past. The people of Flagman's Folly didn't know the full truth behind the fire. A little glow warmed her at the knowledge he had trusted her with his secret. And she would never break his confidence. Still, she couldn't deny her need to learn everything about him that she could.

She was ashamed to admit that need had gone beyond wanting to find something to use against him. It had turned into a strong desire simply to know more about *him*—especially as she now didn't trust anything Ronnie had told her.

Near the barn, a child laughed. A metallic clang rang out, the sound of a horseshoe hitting its mark.

The women drifted into smaller groups. Kayla found herself alone with Ellamae. Before she could say anything, the older woman turned to her.

The court clerk must have taken lessons from the judge. Her own laserlike gaze went through Kayla, too. "Just what are you up to, missy?"

Kayla blinked. "What do you mean?"

"I mean, that phone call I got at the court the other day. Some city dude from up north, asking questions about Sam." She leaned forward. "You wouldn't know anything about that, would you?"

The hair on Kayla's arms prickled. More than likely, the caller had been Matt or one of his associates. But she couldn't know for sure. She shook her head.

"Well, Sam's business is Sam's business, y'hear?"

"I hear," she said agreeably, knowing she shouldn't push the issue right now. Or maybe at all.

Ellamae's attention wandered to the field north of the house. "Looks like we got us a challenge going," she said, effectively changing the subject.

Kayla followed her gaze. Most of the kids, from

kindergartner age on up, had begun to gather in the field.

From across the yard, Kayla caught Becky waving at her. Her niece knew something was up. She curved all her fingers and tapped the tips together, one hand against the other.

Nodding, Kayla repeated the sign. *"Ball."*

After pointing to herself, Becky wiggled her hands, thumbs and pinkies extended. *"Me, play."*

Kayla nodded again. Smiling, she watched Becky run off to join the crowd.

A few of the women drifted over to rest their elbows on the top of the fence separating the field from the yard. Kayla followed.

With the sun now lowering and caught behind one of the clouds, the air was cooler than it had been all day. A light breeze stirred the wild grass growing around the fence posts.

The kids had begun to pick sides for their game. As she waited, Kayla nearly forgot to breathe, feeling as nervous as any mother would to see her child waiting so hopefully to be chosen. Not to be left till last. To her relief, Becky didn't stay on the sidelines for long. Soon, she was out there in the middle of the field, holding her own.

"She's a feisty thing," Ellamae said approvingly.

"How old is she?" asked one of the women.

"Four," Kayla answered.

The woman had a child that age, too. A son. Idly keeping an eye on the kickball game, they shared funny stories and traded helpful hints about raising children, though the other woman did most of the talking.

Kayla knew a lot about Becky's life, but the conversation proved how far she still had to go. What would it be like to know all the details about Becky, the way that woman knew about her son? To be with Becky every day and witness her joy at every new thing she learned?

What had it been like for Sam to miss all those years with her?

No wonder he couldn't forgive Kayla for taking his daughter away.

No wonder he didn't think of her now as anything but unpaid help—and a potential playmate.

Fighting a wave of hopelessness, she forced her attention back to the woman by her side.

Out in the field, the children laughed and shrieked. From the far end of the yard, horseshoes clanged again and again. On the steps of the bunkhouse, Jack sat strumming a guitar.

A loud yell suddenly interrupted the pleasant sounds.

"Hey, why didn't ya look where you were going?" a boy shouted. "We told ya to get out of the way!"

The anger in his voice made Kayla and the other woman look over toward the field. Most of the kids had gathered into a ragged circle in the middle of the play area. A few stragglers ran up to join them.

In the gaps between the children's legs, she could see someone sitting or lying on the ground. Just a brief glimpse of a child's foot covered only by a white ankle sock.

Outside the edge of the circle lay a sneaker, all by itself.

A grass-stained sneaker. Decorated with purple stars.

Chapter Seventeen

If she had ever had any doubts about Sam's genuine concern for his daughter, Kayla certainly didn't hold a single one of them now. As soon as he learned Becky had fallen, he had come running, and he hadn't left her side since.

She sported a scalp wound from her tumble, a minor scrape that bled superficially, nothing more serious than that. She sat in the kitchen for a while with an ice pack pressed against the side of her head, but she soon wanted to give that up in her eagerness to go back outside again.

"Play?" she signed to Kayla. *"Me, play?"*

The kickball game had ended, and the kids Becky's age had turned their attention to the plastic horseshoes set up alongside the barn.

At Kayla's nod, Becky ran from the room, banging the kitchen door behind her.

Kayla turned to Sam, who looked more upset than the child herself. "It's okay," she reassured him. "Just a minor accident."

"I realize that." Looking puzzled, he shook his head. "But I don't get it. You didn't want her up on a horse—which is something she could learn to handle without having to say a word." He gestured widely toward the door. "Yet it's okay to have her out there on that field with a bunch of kids running around her, in a situation she can't control."

"That's different."

"How?"

She frowned at him. "All kids learn to play with others, Sam. Sometimes the games are physical, and they're rough. And sometimes the kids get knocked down or hurt in the process. You must know that—you were a kid once yourself. It's natural."

"Yeah? Well, out here, it's natural to spend half your life on the back of a horse." He followed in Becky's wake, letting the screen door slam closed even more loudly than she had done.

The finality of the sound underscored what Sam had left unsaid. She had no doubt it also reinforced her thoughts.

When it came to Becky, the two of them would never find a middle ground.

STANDING IN THE AFTERNOON shadows on the east side of the barn, Sam swung his ax against the rotted tree stump, again and again. He'd put off getting rid of this stump for a long while, but somehow, today seemed like the right time to do the job. Hot and tiring work, but not as hot as he felt inside.

Almost a week had passed since the get-together with the folks from town. He had gone back to working his ranch but had stuck close to the house, often bringing Becky to the barn with him while he'd taken care of chores there.

He kept thinking back to that afternoon of the barbecue, though. The day had about come to an end, as it was. Just the second round of desserts, the gathering up of dishes and kids, and the goodbyes. Becky had to spend part of that time with an ice pack resting on the scrape on her head. Still, she didn't seem bothered by it.

And that wasn't what made him hot under the collar now.

He took another whack at the stump and left the ax buried deep. Like the feelings he'd been trying to hide. Guilt and anger and a whole lot more.

Luckily, Becky's fall had been exactly what Kayla had said, nothing more than an accident. The problem was, he should have been watching his daughter himself, instead of trying to stay away from Kayla. Sitting on the bench beside her that afternoon had made him see things more clearly. Had made him glad to run off to throw a few horseshoes.

Why had he been avoiding her, and not keeping an eye on his child? Because of the way Kayla took care of Becky. Because of her insistence on teaching him to sign. Because of their near kiss on the couch. And because of the kiss they *had* shared. Put all that together, and you had the truth right there.

Yeah, sitting next to her that afternoon had given him a heads-up. Had made him realize he'd fallen for the woman who wanted to take his child away.

Kayla was right. He really *was* crazy.

He yanked his bandanna from his jeans pocket and dragged it across his brow. If only he could erase the thoughts inside his head just as easily as he wiped away the sweat outside.

As he lowered the cloth from his face, he saw Kayla standing by the corner of the barn. She hadn't been there a minute ago. But she sure was there now, standing with her hands tucked into the pockets of her denim shorts.

He got rid of the bandanna. Grabbed the handle of the ax and started to work it out of the wood. Anything to keep from looking at her.

"Sam."

So she wasn't going away. He shrugged. It was as good a time as any to let her know the decision he'd made. He gave the stump another ferocious wallop. Finally, he met her eyes. "Your way isn't going to work, Kayla. No matter how much you want it to."

"What do you mean?"

"I've learned a lot besides those few signs you've shown me. Being with Becky has taught me she needs to be with people who can communicate with her, who can take care of her full-time. In her language."

"That," she said forcefully, "is what I've told you all along. It's exactly why I want her home in Chicago with me."

"Not if I have something to say about it. Besides, that still wouldn't be enough." He shook his head. "Face it, Kayla. She needs more than I can give her. More than even you can provide. She needs a dozen of you in her life, every day."

The idea had been nagging at him all these weeks now, and seeing Becky lying on that field the day of the barbecue had only brought it home to him. "She ought to be surrounded by friends who can talk with her and play with her in a way they can *all* understand. So that no one, including Becky, will get hurt like she did that day."

"It was only an accident, Sam."

"Yes, I know that. It was also the spur I needed to get me moving."

He could see her back straighten, her shoulders stiffen. "Moving toward what?"

"Toward doing what I need to for Becky." He yanked the ax free. "You don't have to worry about her, about her classes, or about her having an interpreter. I'm going to get her everything she needs."

Even in the shadows, he saw her face pale. But she fought back.

"You're getting ahead of things, aren't you? After all, Judge Baylor—"

"Saw exactly what happened that afternoon. Don't even think twice about what the judge's verdict will be. I'm not. And I've made my decision." He tossed the ax onto the pile of wood in the wheelbarrow. "I'm sending Becky to a school where she'll stay with other deaf kids."

"A residential school? You mean, you would send her to live away from you?"

He nodded shortly. It was the hardest decision he'd ever made. "Look, in these weeks, I've gotten close to Becky. And she's come to trust me. All the more reason for me to do the right thing by her. For once in her life."

He started down the length of the barn, knowing he would have to go past her. Deliberately, he kept his gaze on the loaded wheelbarrow. He didn't want to look at her. Didn't want to see the expression on her face. As he came near, she held up her hand. He wasn't sure what he would do if she tried to touch him. Fight like hell not to take her in his arms, probably. He stopped beside her but stared across the yard.

"Sam."

He tried to tune her out. How she felt shouldn't matter to him. Becky was his daughter, and only he had the right to decide what was best for her. Over at the house, he could see her sitting on the top porch step.

"Look at her," he said, his voice raspy, his throat tight.

Kayla turned slowly away from him and faced the yard.

Becky sat playing with the stuffed lamb he'd bought for her. With her free hand, she sketched words in the air.

"She needs people around her who can talk to her that way," he said urgently to Kayla. "Real people. *Friends.* Not just dolls and stuffed animals." He hardened his heart and his voice and demanded, "How can you say you care about her but not be willing to give her that?"

Now he couldn't help looking at Kayla, couldn't help seeing her blank, wide-eyed expression. She looked shell-shocked.

Before she could respond, he walked away, clamping his jaw shut against a whole list of other things he wanted to tell her. Why bother to share any of that? She wouldn't be around long enough to make it worth his while.

Besides, the look on her face just now had told him she wouldn't accept *any* of his ideas.

LATER THAT NIGHT, KAYLA paced the floor of her bedroom, her cell phone clutched in her hand. Her thumbs sped across the keypad as she tapped out a message almost faster than she could think, making up for her lack of reaction earlier. Too little, much too late.

Sam's announcement had hit her like a physical blow. His news had stunned her so completely, she couldn't summon words to respond to him. Couldn't make herself move quickly enough to stop him before he walked away.

Couldn't find the courage, for a few long, heartbreaking moments, even to turn and look at her niece.

How could she have let things come to this? How could she have failed Becky this way?

Her thumb stabbed at the send button.

When Lianne responded almost in the space of a heartbeat, Kayla could have cried with relief.

Can't Matt do something? Lianne texted.

Kayla groaned. I called him. He's not answering his phones, cell or home. I'll bet Kerry's gone into labor. I didn't even leave a message. But I'm sure if he'd found out anything, he would have been in touch already. She choked back a panicked sob. It's too late. He hasn't turned up anything we can use to fight with. And I'm not doing any better at this end.

The only things she did know—about the fire and Sam's wild past—couldn't help her.

She *had* to get custody of Becky. And she would.

Still, there was the fear. The chance. The slim possibility she didn't want to think about, that the judge would rule against her. And if she waited until he had made his decision, only to find her fears had come true, it would be too late for her to press Sam for a better solution.

Too late to do anything at all.

Lianne, what if I DON'T get custody?

She gripped the phone more tightly and felt thankful for the silent communication. If she'd had to say those words aloud, everyone in Flagman's Folly would have heard her.

That won't happen, Lianne shot back.

It could. And then he'll send Becky off to school.
She'll be all alone. And scared. You know she will.
You know that more than anyone.

Kayla, I hate to say this but...

Lianne's message trailed off, as if she was choosing
her next words carefully.

She froze. Now what? Had Ronnie turned up? Was
there even more bad news? Before she could tap out her
question, her phone vibrated. Lianne again.

I think having me go away to school was harder on
you than on me.

What are you saying?

I had friends at school. I was happy there.

You wanted to come home to us!

A pause, while Kayla held her breath. And then a
long message from Lianne.

Yes, I wanted to come home to you all. But I have to
be honest—I wanted to finish up my last few years
of school at home, too. Being mainstreamed for
high school wouldn't have been right for a lot of my
friends, but it was the right thing for me.

Kayla tapped furiously at her keys. That's what I feel
for Becky. It's all about what's right for her. And it's not
right for her father to send her away to school.

Then, Lianne said simply, you need to convince Sam
not to do that.

WITH ONLY THE FEW SCATTERED hours of sleep she'd managed to get, Kayla felt grateful when Sam stayed quiet all through breakfast the next morning. She did need to talk to him, but first, she had to get her sleep-deprived brain to cooperate with her.

After they'd finished eating, Sam suddenly announced he was spending the day with Jack and his cowboys out in the high pastures.

Wherever they might be.

He was across the kitchen and out the door to the back porch before she could blink. Through the window over the sink, she saw him striding rapidly toward his truck.

She swallowed her surprise and tried to gather her thoughts before he had time to drive away.

"I'll be right back," she said to Sharleen and Becky.

By the time she reached the porch, he had already opened the driver's door.

"Sam, wait," she called. She hurried across the yard. "I wanted to talk to you about what you said yesterday. About sending Becky to school. *If* you do get custody of her, I hope you won't go through with that. Not right away."

He frowned. "What good is delaying it going to do? She needs to go to school. They said she needs to be keeping up with the signs she knows, and learning more."

"That's true," she acknowledged, unable to deny it. He'd done his homework, all right. "But Becky's been with you for such a short time. Sam—" She swallowed, her mouth so dry it felt as though she'd just sliced her throat with a knife. She didn't want to force her words past the pain. She didn't want to say them at all. But she had to. *If* she didn't get custody, she had to make sure Sam did what was right for her niece. "Becky needs stability. She needs to be with her daddy."

He looked at her for a long time, his eyes almost liquid silver in the early-morning sun. "She needs to be with people she can communicate with," he said emphatically. "The school is a great place for her. She'll be able to learn in her own language and have plenty of kids to play with." He looked away, his jaw set firmly.

At the sound of the screen door slapping against the jamb, they both turned their gazes toward the house. Becky stood on the porch, several dolls and stuffed animals cradled in her arms.

As they watched, she came down the steps and went over near the barn to the play area she had claimed for her own.

"What Becky needs," Sam said finally, his voice hoarse, "is that school. You ought to want that for her, too."

She turned to him. "I *do* want it. I want everything for her, and more. And the school would be a wonderful place for her. I agree with you on that, too. But there will be time for the school later, if you still feel you want to send her away."

Impulsively, she put her hand on his arm. He jerked at her touch, his muscles tightening beneath her palm. She dropped her hand and stepped back. She wanted to convince him of her sincerity, not drive him away.

Already, he had shifted closer to the driver's seat.

As if keeping herself physically near would help close the emotional distance between them, she gripped the inside handle of the open door.

"Sam, please," she said, finally driven to begging. That didn't matter. "She's so young, and her life has been nothing but a series of upsets since she was born. Nothing has been stable for her. Ever."

She had to admit the truth. To tell Sam everything, so she could make him understand.

"My parents and sister and I love Becky. We take care of her whenever she's with us. But as often as that is, it isn't the same for her as having a permanent home. We can't always be there when she needs us. When Ronnie takes her away." Again, that knife seemed to slice her throat. Her voice grew as hoarse as Sam's. "Becky needs to know that she can count on the people around her to be there for her, always. She needs to feel that her life is secure. But if you get custody and send her away, Becky won't even have that."

Sam looked off into the distance, where the horizon was broken by a series of tree-covered hills.

When he finally turned back to look at her, his eyes seemed nearly bottomless, darkened by an emotion she couldn't read. He leaned toward her, held out one hand as if planning to touch her, then finally rested it on the door handle, his fingers brushing hers. She could tell he hadn't noticed the contact.

He sighed. "You know I can't be here for her every minute, Kayla. No one can. That's an impossible thing to ask." He climbed into the truck and tugged at the door.

Feeling the gap between them widen, she dropped her hand. Physically, they were inches away from each other. Emotionally, they had taken stances wider apart than the walls of one of the arroyos that left deep cracks in Sam's land.

"I'm doing what I have to do." After starting the engine, he pulled the door closed.

As he shifted into gear, Kayla backed a step, then

another. He swung the truck in an arc and pulled out of the yard.

By the barn, Becky watched the truck disappear down the road. Then she looked over at Kayla and raised her brows. She gestured, touching all her fingertips together and dragging her hand through the air. *"Go away?"*

Kayla nodded.

Becky moved that hand to her temple and brushed her fingers downward. *"Why?"* She wrinkled her forehead, puzzled.

No wonder, when Sam had been spending so much time with her lately. Becky wasn't used to having him leave her behind.

Kayla sighed. She signed *"Daddy,"* then tapped her right fist on the back of her left one. *"Work."*

But it wasn't work, Kayla knew. Not completely.

He'd left so abruptly to get away from *her*. To keep from having to listen to what she had to say. She looked down the road at the billowing dust kicked up by his truck in his haste to put space between them.

She clenched her fists, and her temper flared.

For a man who worried so much about his daughter being able to communicate, he wasn't so hot at conversation himself.

Abruptly, she relaxed her fingers. She couldn't hide from herself any longer. Time to think about what had really gotten her so uptight. What had kept her awake those last few hours before dawn had started to break.

Sam claimed he was doing what he had to do. Doing the right thing for Becky.

Kayla thought of her conversation with Lianne the night before. Lianne had given her full support. She'd only briefly mentioned the benefit of finishing her schooling in a mainstream school. What she *hadn't* said was one word about the countless benefits she'd had in her earlier years, growing up around kids who spoke the same language she did.

Exactly Sam's argument.

And the root of Kayla's newest fear.

She loved Becky more than anything in the world. But in her determination to win custody, had she lost sight of what was best for her niece?

Even with his inexperience and lack of knowledge of his daughter's life, did Sam have the right idea all along?

Chapter Eighteen

Much as she believed Sam about Ronnie's stories, Kayla now couldn't doubt the ones Ronnie had told her about his obsessive hours spent on the ranch. Since the day of their argument a week before over sending Becky to school, he had disappeared before sunrise every morning and hadn't come home again until dinner.

Through the kitchen window, Kayla watched Becky in the backyard, playing with Pirate. Sam would have a fit if he knew the dog still came to visit the ranch every day. But how could he know?

Besides, Becky missed her daddy, and the puppy made a good distraction.

Kayla wouldn't admit that she missed Sam, too.

Yet, maybe it was better this way. The distance between them now would make the permanent separation easier—for all of them.

Tomorrow marked the end of their six weeks. They would go to the courtroom at Town Hall, where Judge Baylor would make his decision.

A short while later, when the cell phone she had left on the kitchen counter rang, Kayla had her hands filled with the vegetables she'd just taken out of the crisper. She dropped them into the sink and hurried across the room.

Seeing the Chicago exchange on the display, she grabbed at the phone and flipped it open. Had Matt finally found some information she could use to take to the judge?

"It's a girl!" he said joyfully.

"Oh, Matt, that's wonderful!" Even as she congratulated him, she had to fight the sinking feeling in the pit of her stomach.

"Six pounds, eight ounces," he went on, "and I know you won't believe this, but she's got red hair like Kerry."

She laughed. "Told you so. With all the redheads in her family, you didn't stand a chance."

"I know. Well, I can live with it."

"I'm sure. What's her name?"

"We're still trying to decide. It's turned into a family matter. Kerry's brothers are trying to round up votes for their choices. Her uncle claims since he brought us together, Kerry and I should name the baby after him. I don't think so."

"Maybe not," she agreed. "Well, give her a hug from me and tell her I'll see you all soon." Too soon.

Her heart throbbed painfully. What had been only a thought in her mind a few minutes ago had turned into stark reality now that she'd given voice to it. She looked through the kitchen window and over toward the barn, where Becky appeared to be putting the dog through his paces.

She *would* be home again, very soon. The question was, after the hearing was over, would she be taking Becky back with her? "Can't wait to see the baby," she added, forcing a lightness she didn't feel into her tone. "Congratulations again."

"Thanks," Matt said. "But, Kayla, that's not the only reason I called."

"Oh?" She gripped the phone tighter.

"First item, we've reached Ronnie. She was off to the Bahamas with a friend. A female friend. Whatever wedding plans she had were called off, and she said she's not getting remarried after all. But she has confirmed that she's given custody of Becky to Robertson. Permanently. And she's willing to sign any paperwork necessary."

Kayla sighed. "Well, at least we know."

Now she only needed to fight Sam.

"Second item," Matt continued. "We've gotten some updated reports on Robertson. They show he's been working to pay off a lot of outstanding credit card bills. Very large bills."

"Where did he get the money?"

"He's sold some of his stock—animal stock, that is—in the past couple of weeks. And he's planning to put part of his property up for sale."

She gasped. Through the window, she looked at the barn and at the tree-covered hills in the distance. Sam loved this ranch. He wouldn't part with any of it, she knew. Not unless he had dire reasons for it. "Why?" she asked Matt. "Do you know?"

He hesitated.

It wasn't like him not to be up-front about anything. "What is it?"

"I don't know this for sure." He sounded troubled. "But he could want to show he's solvent when he presents his case to the judge."

"Solvent?"

"Yes. He could use his newly inflated bank account to prove he has the means to take care of Becky financially."

"And I don't," she said dully.

"We both know what a teacher's salary is like."

"We do." She swallowed a sigh. "Well, thanks for letting me know, Matt. And again, hugs for Kerry and the baby."

When they ended the call, she sat with the phone still clutched in her hand.

The news from Matt had shaken her. Badly.

She would give Becky all the love and care in the world, but when it came to finances, she couldn't compete with a rancher's income. Especially with the additional amounts Sam's land would bring in.

If the judge took Sam's assets into consideration, he would never rule in her favor. She would never win custody of Becky.

She would have to face making the trip home to Chicago alone.

His footsteps dragging, Sam crossed the yard, headed toward the house. It was getting on time for supper, and he wanted to prolong the minutes before he would have to go in and sit down at the table.

And he knew full well why.

In the weeks that Kayla had been on his ranch, even with all the upset between them, he felt closer to her, felt more of the joy a real family could bring, than he ever had with his ex. But he couldn't get used to those things. Couldn't let himself get any more wrapped up in Kayla. Couldn't dwell on what *he* wanted anymore.

The judge had shot a long-held belief out from under him earlier this week.

Kayla would shoot one of his dreams dead, too, when she left him.

A full week of keeping himself busy away from the

ranch house and far from her hadn't provided the time he needed to come to terms with it all.

He'd missed Kayla more than he should have this week.

He'd missed Becky, too. Every night, he made sure to talk with her before bedtime, at least as much as he could with his limited vocabulary. Though he now spent his evenings in the office, thumbing through the sign language dictionary, the solitary study sessions weren't enough.

And not nearly as much fun as learning from Kayla.

As he approached the house, she came to the back door and looked at him through the screen. She nodded shortly. "You're later than usual."

"Had to hoist a lost calf out of an arroyo," he said. "Filthy job. I showered out in the bunkhouse."

"Do they get lost like that often?" she asked.

"Often enough." He braced one booted foot on the second step and leaned against the railing. Delaying, just as he'd done with the shower.

"Time for Becky to come in and wash up yet?" he asked.

"Yes. She's over by the barn. But—"

"I'll get her."

"Sam, wait." When he stopped, she hesitated, then continued. "She's playing with Pirate."

"Don't I know it." He could tell he'd surprised her with the news. Did she think he didn't know what went on around here? "I've seen the mutt hanging around every night when I come home." Turning back, he headed toward the west side of the yard. He'd only made it halfway to the barn when Becky ran from around the corner of it. The dog bounded at her heels.

Before he could say a word or do anything to chase the animal off, Becky raised her hand and tapped her thumb against her chin. She held her first two fingers in a *V* near her cheek, forming the sign he'd once playfully used with Kayla.

"Daddy, see."

His chest swelled with emotion, and hell, with a little pride, too. He could understand his daughter. He could talk with her.

"Okay," he signed, and waited.

She turned and clapped her hands, and the dog sank to his haunches.

Next, she raised her hands in the air, palms skyward, and the puppy sat up and begged.

Finally, she swung one hand in a huge circle, and that darned pup rolled over on his back in the dirt and lay there till she'd given him a belly rub.

Becky's laughter almost drowned out the sound of the puppy's barks.

Sam shook his head. "All right, that's it."

He turned abruptly and nearly crashed into Kayla. He'd been so caught up in the performance, he hadn't noticed she had come down from the porch and moved to stand almost beside him.

Her eyes wide, she said urgently, "Pirate's the only friend Becky gets to play with out here. I know you don't like Porter, and with good reason. *Very* good reason. But that doesn't mean you need to cut Becky off from playing with the puppy."

Nodding, he waved Becky over to him. When she came to his side, he took her by the hand and led her to his pickup.

"Sam?" Kayla came up behind them. "Where are you going?"

He gave her a long, thoughtful look before replying. "Why don't you come along and see?" he asked. "Instead of jumping to conclusions?"

KAYLA WATCHED SAM SETTLE Becky in the backseat of his truck. Then, to her surprise, he opened the tailgate and allowed Pirate to jump onto the flatbed. He probably wanted to make darn sure the pup went back to his own home.

Unless he planned to take him somewhere else and drop him off.

Her heart told her he wouldn't do a thing like that. But obviously, he also didn't plan to give Kayla an explanation. And he didn't plan to wait. If she wanted to know what he was up to, she would have to go along for the ride.

After a word to Sam, she ran into the house to let Sharleen know they were leaving, then she dashed back out to the truck.

They made a short, quiet trip to the neighboring ranch. She spent most of it looking over her shoulder, watching her niece sign to Pirate through the back window of the truck's cab.

When they reached Porter's house, Sam let the dog out.

Pirate barked and jumped up and down beside the truck, trying to get to Becky, who was struggling to unfasten her seat belt. Kayla shook her head at Becky. Who knew what would happen between Sam and Porter, and she didn't want her niece anywhere near them.

She lowered her passenger window so she could hear whatever went on.

A moment later, the front door swung open and Porter

came out onto the porch, glaring at Sam. "What do you want?"

"It's about time we had a talk."

"Got nothing to say to you, Sam."

"Well, I've got something to say to you."

Porter's hands closed into fists.

Kayla yanked the door handle and pushed so hard that when the door flew open, she nearly tumbled to the ground.

"Sam." She hurried over to him.

He put out a hand to stop her and said to the other man, "About that dog out there by my truck."

Porter looked over at the puppy and laughed. "Can't complain about the mutt now. He's on my land, not yours. Which reminds me, I thought you swore never to set foot on this property again."

"You thought wrong. I swore only one thing when it came to you, and you know what that was."

"Yeah." Porter nodded.

"I kept your secret all these years. But I hear you're not so good about keeping your mouth shut."

Kayla edged forward, holding her breath. What did that mean?

Porter laughed. "Well, you know how it is when a man gets a little too much drink in him."

"I know when a *boy* does it," Sam corrected.

Porter ignored that. "So, who told you? Ellamae, our esteemed town clerk and town crier?"

"The judge."

Kayla frowned. When had he been talking to the judge? And what else had they discussed? She pushed the questions away. She would deal with them later. Right now, she needed to focus on this conversation.

"You've been nothing but pond scum, Porter, ever

since that day in your daddy's barn. Maybe even before." Sam stepped forward. "I think you owe me. And I think we ought to settle things right now. Nothing's going to pay me back for what I did for you. But give me the mutt, and we'll call it even."

"What?" The man's tone said clearly that he thought Sam was out of his mind.

Kayla had once thought so, too. She clasped her hands together, fighting to hold on to her emotions.

"I don't like you much," Sam said, his voice calm and steady.

She could hear the venom in his tone, but she never once felt the need to move away. Becky was safe. Sam wouldn't hurt that man.

"My daughter's taken a liking to your dog," he continued. "Let me have the pup, and we'll keep our past where it belongs."

Shrugging, Porter shifted his gaze away from them. "Sure, Sam. Take the mutt with you right now."

Sam turned, waving Kayla ahead of him.

Becky was all smiles when he let Pirate jump into the back of the truck again.

"Sam—" Kayla began.

"Wait till we get away from this scum," he said tersely.

Not until Porter's house was merely a speck in her side-view mirror did Sam say another word. As he spoke, he turned his head to look at her. "Did you think I was going to hit Porter?"

"No," she said immediately. And truthfully. "Now who's jumping to conclusions? That wasn't about protecting Becky. I knew you wouldn't touch him. But after what happened outside the barbershop that day, I was afraid he might hit *you.*"

He looked away again, nodding, but said nothing.

She took a deep breath. "I am confused, though. What was all that about Judge Baylor?"

Sam's laugh sounded bitter. "He told me he'd been at one of our local saloons a long while back and had come across Porter there. The man started talking and never stopped."

"About that night?"

"Yep."

"And he was under the influence?"

"I believe so. Though, it might've been just the *judge's* influence." He shook his head. "That man's got a way of getting things out of a person that they don't even know are in them."

Kayla felt a chill, and not just from the breeze coming in the window she had forgotten to close. "When did you and the judge talk about all this?" she asked in what she hoped was a casual tone.

"Last week. I ran across him when I went in to the feed store."

What else had they talked about?

Kayla wanted desperately to know. Yet she couldn't bring herself to ask the question. She came up with another one instead. "What exactly did Porter tell the judge?"

"It was more like the judge told him." He said nothing else. They'd reached the road to the house. He drove along silently and parked the truck in its usual spot near the barn.

When he had climbed out, he released Becky from her booster seat and Pirate from the back of the truck. The two of them ran across the yard.

Sam rounded the back of the truck and headed toward the house.

"Sam."

He stopped and turned back to her.

"What did the judge tell Porter?" Suddenly, she had to know.

Sam looked off into the distance. "Seems like Porter's been running his mouth for years about everything under the sun. Including what happened in the barn that night."

"You mean...?"

"He suckered me in, and then he went off and bragged about what he'd done and how he'd gotten me to cover for him." He shook his head. "I've spent more than a decade keeping his secret. Keeping up that lie. But one night he got drunk in town—not long after it happened, either—and he spilled everything to one of his so-called buddies." He laughed bitterly. "And you know how talk spreads around here."

She did.

"All those years," he said softly, "I lived with that lie. And all the while, everyone in town knew the truth."

Her chest tightened and she inhaled a long, shaky breath.

She'd tried so hard in these weeks with Sam to keep thinking of him as the man who wanted to steal her beloved niece away. As the enemy. But, little by little, his actions had chipped away at that image. His concern for Becky. His willingness, finally, to learn to sign. The agreement he had just made about the puppy.

And now, his reaction over learning he'd been betrayed.

She wanted to throw herself into his arms and make him forget about the past. Help him erase that decade's worth of deceit he'd been forced to bear.

Not good, when she'd just cautioned herself about keeping her distance from him.

But she had to do something.

"Let it go, Sam," she murmured. "Porter's not worth it. You *are*. And isn't it better that everyone knows you're a man to be trusted?"

"Everyone?"

Both his tone and his unyielding expression froze her in place. Could he mean her? But she did trust him. She knew he didn't lie. She knew he wasn't violent. She knew she could trust him with anything...

Except the one thing she valued most.

Nothing in the world could make her tell him that.

As if he already knew, he nodded and walked away.

"Sam." She still couldn't share what she'd been thinking, but she couldn't let him leave with those unspoken words between them.

He turned back, his eyes dark, his face drawn, closed in.

She took a deep breath. "I wanted to thank you," she said softly. "For taking Pirate in. Becky just loves that dog."

"Yeah?" He looked over toward the barn. "Not as much as I love Becky."

Chapter Nineteen

Later that night, with Sam in his office and Becky safely tucked into bed, Kayla stole away to her borrowed room and curled up on the bed.

She'd tried her best to focus on Sharleen during dinner. To keep up a conversation with the other woman and avoid watching Becky and Sam. It hurt to see them together. It hurt to come to this room alone and know she would never share a bed with Sam. Everything hurt.

Except knowing Sam's true feelings for his daughter.

She shouldn't have been surprised to hear that he loved his child. He had always wanted to do what was best for Becky.

He was a good man.

Even knowing where Pirate had come from, Sam had accepted the dog. Had negotiated for the puppy, giving up something of himself in the process. Just as, for all those years, he had kept the promise he'd made to a friend, despite the sacrifices he'd had to live with.

Life was full of sacrifices.

Full of compromises, too, as she had heard from Lianne the day the judge had ordered them into this arrangement. She had been right about that.

Now Kayla was going to offer Sam a compromise she hoped he could live with.

Just before she made the ultimate sacrifice herself.

Only one thing in all this mess had brought her even a glimmer of happiness. With shaking fingers, she tapped out a message to Lianne on the keypad of her phone.

I've done some research at this end. There's a charter school in the area, not an hour away from here.

Sounds good.

A charter school for deaf AND hearing students. They have resource and mainstream classes. Becky will be able to sign all day. And she'll be able to be home every night.

Great!

Yes. She had left the information in a highly visible place on Sam's desk. If only he would agree to the change in schools. He still might balk, but she had to hope his concern would override any roadblocks.

She read Lianne's next text. It's the perfect solution for Becky and Sam. But what about you?

Kayla sighed. I can't fight Sam anymore over custody. His admission of how much he loved Becky had stolen her breath. I can't try to take her away from him. She's already a part of her daddy's heart. She needs to be a part of his life, too. No matter how much it hurt her to admit it, she knew the truth in her own heart at last. Becky belongs with Sam.

Kayla would have to go home alone. She would have

to leave behind not one, but the two people she most loved in the world.

And there was no sense at all in trying to convince Sam to let her have visitation rights with Becky. Recalling the look on his face that afternoon, when she couldn't speak the words to tell him she trusted him completely, told her she would get nowhere with that. She'd have better luck attempting to twist the judge around her little finger.

But she had to try. Had to hope Sam could find some compassion in his heart for her.

Even more important, she had to hope he'd be openminded enough to consider an alternative for Becky.

BREAKFAST WAS ANOTHER awkward meal, except for Becky's excited laughter as she told them all about Pirate's night in the barn. How she knew all this, Sam hadn't a clue, but he listened eagerly as Kayla relayed the story.

Someday, he'd be able to figure out *all* Becky's words himself.

If only he could figure out a few other things now. If only he didn't have even more worries to think about. Since finding the paperwork Kayla had left on his desk the night before, his thoughts had become more confused than ever.

Kayla's arguments about Becky staying with him had stuck in his mind and wouldn't let go.

Becky needs to know that she can count on the people around her to be there for her, always.

His daughter could count on him, forever. He'd sworn it.

But Kayla had talked about stability for Becky, too, and the child's need for a permanent home. He couldn't help thinking of the way Ronnie had dropped Becky off on him. Had abandoned her.

By sending his child away to school, would he be abandoning her, too?

The phone rang, and he rose to answer it. The real estate company, looking for the go-ahead to advertise his land.

"Don't do anything yet," he told the woman. "I'm holding off on putting those acres up for sale. If I decide to go ahead with it, I'll get back to you." When he finished the call and returned to his place at the table, he found Kayla looking at him curiously.

"You're selling some of your land?" she asked.

"Maybe."

"Why? I thought you loved this ranch."

"I do. I like keeping it up, too, and paying my ranch hands on time. I like eating regularly. And taking care of my own." He looked over at Becky. "But it's kind of hard to handle all that when the debt collectors are standing with their hands out."

Her shocked look seemed a little forced. "I'm surprised you'd let yourself get into that kind of trouble."

"*I* didn't."

"Then…" She paused. "You mean, Ronnie?"

"No one else."

"Oh, Sam. I'm sorry…" She stopped.

The sudden glimmer in her eyes had him shoving himself to his feet. He stood there for a long moment, fighting to keep from reaching out to her.

After everything they'd been through these weeks, and considering what they were facing today, she still had some kind of compassion for him.

Her reaction only added another layer of confusion onto his already mixed-up thoughts.

Yesterday, at Porter's, she hadn't been trying to stop him from fighting, as he'd first believed. She had been trying to protect him against the man. Same as she'd done that day in town, out in front of Joe's barbershop. Same as she'd done that day—and every day—for Becky, even to the point of trying to protect his daughter from *him*.

How could he hurt a woman like this?

And how could he ever have thought he'd be worthy of her?

"Yeah," he said, finally. "I'm sorry, too."

THE FAN ABOVE THE JUDGE's desk whirred, sending a breeze through the courtroom. The cooler air did nothing to take the moisture from Sam's brow. He'd made his plans, and he was going through with them.

"All right." The judge tapped his gavel on the desktop. "Court's in session. Let's get things taken care of." Smiling, he looked at Sam and Kayla. "From information received, I can happily say you've both followed my suggestion to come together to bond with that little girl."

Suggestion? Sam nearly laughed. What would the man's orders sound like?

"Now, I guess it's time to state my opinion in this matter."

"Your Honor," Kayla said. "Before you do, I'd like to speak."

The judge frowned. Sam looked at her in surprise. Across the room, he saw Ellamae's jaw drop.

Kayla cleared her throat. "I want to give up my request for custody of Becky."

This time, Sam's jaw dropped. He shut it again and

shook his head. He couldn't have heard that right. "What did you say?"

"I want to give up my request for custody," she repeated. She crossed her arms. "But I'm not leaving here until you agree to give me visitation—"

"How often?" he demanded.

Her shoulders went back, but she stood her ground. "Twice a year."

"Twice?" He frowned. "Are you kidding me?"

"No. I'm not going to settle for less than that, Sam. And I want—"

Bang!

Startled, they turned to the judge.

"You'll pardon me," he drawled, "but I do have the peculiar habit of liking to participate in my own hearings." He gestured with the gavel. "Why don't you two step out in the hall? Come on back when you've talked things over some."

"All right, Judge," Sam said. "But sit tight. We'll be right with you." Taking Kayla by the hand, he towed her down the aisle and out of the courtroom. In the hall, he released her. "Is that really all you want to see of Becky?" he demanded. "Two times a year will satisfy you?"

Tears shimmered in her eyes.

"I thought not," he said softly. "That's not what I want, either."

"What do you want?" she asked, her voice shaking.

"First, for you to understand I wouldn't do anything to hurt you. But I have to think of Becky, too. I truly believe a school where she will be able to sign is the best place for her." He took a deep breath, then let it out again. "I checked out the info you left on the desk. About the charter school. I talked to a few people this morning. They gave it a good rating. And I want her to sleep in her own bed every night. I agree—it's exactly the *right* place for Becky."

A tear ran down her cheek. He wiped it away with a trembling finger.

"And…" He took another deep breath. "I agree with you about Becky needing stability. From both of us. When she comes home every day, I want you to be there."

"I know." Her voice broke. "You want me to stay permanently. You said that once before."

"That's not what I mean now, not at all. I'd planned to say this to you in front of the judge before we heard his decision. You just beat me to the punch." She stood looking at him, not saying a word. Not giving him an inch. That didn't bother him. He'd go miles for this woman, if he had to.

He swallowed hard. "Kayla, from the day I burned down that barn, it seemed like my life was worthless. Like I had to spend it doing everything the hard way. The wrong way. Drinking and running wild and just plain making a fool of myself. When I finally got straight again, I hated every part of my past. But I don't hate it anymore."

This time, his voice broke. "I can't regret a single thing about the way my life went after that night in the barn. It brought me Becky. And it brought me you."

Her eyes shimmered again with tears, giving him hope.

"Marry me, Kayla." He dug into his pocket and held out his hand. On his palm lay the diamond ring he'd bought days ago. "I love you. Becky loves you. Our lives won't be complete without you. We need to be a real family. Together." When she said nothing, he nodded.

"I know it's too soon for you to hear this. But I don't want to lose you, ever. *Either* of you.

"Give the idea some thought." His laugh sounded as shaky as his voice had a moment ago. "If I can learn to sign with Becky, maybe you can learn to love me."

"No," she said softly, "it's too late."

For a moment, he felt his heart stop. Then it started up again, just as strong and steady as his determination. He couldn't settle for her answer. He wouldn't. "I thought it was too late when it came to learning to talk to my own daughter. But you proved me wrong." Though he clenched his fist around the ring, he barely felt the diamond biting into his palm. "Give me some time to prove myself to you."

She shook her head. "I don't need time. I need you."

The words rocked him nearly off his feet. He filled his chest with a breath so deep, he thought the snaps on his Western shirt would fly open.

"It's too late to learn to love you, Sam, because I already do."

He tilted his head and narrowed his eyes, but he couldn't hold back a smile. "And were you planning to tell me, someday?"

"I…" She turned her head away.

Gently, he touched her chin and turned her to face him again. "What is it?"

"I thought…with our history. With all the stories I'd believed from…" She trailed off again.

"No need to think about that at all. That's one part of the past I've already forgotten," he told her honestly. "You're the only woman for me, Kayla. And the only mother I want for Becky—and for the rest of our kids." He opened his arms wide.

"The rest—?" Even as she laughed, she shook her head. "Hold on a minute there, cowboy. It sounds like you've got a long-term plan."

"Not long-term. Permanent."

"In that case, shouldn't we make it official, too?" She wiggled the fingers of her left hand.

"We should." He motioned for Becky to join them. She stood by his side, watching wide-eyed as he slipped the solitaire onto Kayla's ring finger. "Kayla, will you marry us?"

Looking at Becky, she signed the words and explained their meaning. It pleased him to have her think of his daughter right away. It pleased him just as much to see Becky grin.

Finally, Kayla turned back to Sam and bobbed her fist in the air emphatically. *"Yes!"*

This time, when he held his arms wide, she stepped into his embrace without a moment's hesitation.

From the corner of his eye, he saw Becky waving her hands in the silent gesture of applause.

Epilogue

One month later

Kayla looked around the café.

She and Sam, Dori had assured them, would have the best wedding reception Flagman's Folly had ever seen, right there at the Double S.

She'd certainly lived up to her promise.

Tables and chairs had been rearranged to create a spacious dance floor. Food and drink appeared without end. The doors and windows had been flung wide to let in the music from the quartet playing out on the patio. The mixture of mariachi tunes and old favorites kept everyone dancing.

Kayla's parents took yet another turn around the room. Over in one corner, Lianne was holding court, with a couple of cowboys around her and Jack standing in the wings.

At the edge of the dance floor, Sam stood holding Becky's hand.

Her heart swelling, Kayla watched him go down on one knee before Becky.

In halting but clear signs, he told her that they were now one family. *"Daddy. Mommy-Kayla. And Becky."*

Her niece—no. *Their daughter* reached up and

wrapped her hands around Sam's neck. He rose and swung in a circle, holding Becky close. When he set her on the floor again, they exchanged a special message. Kayla had taught Sam the signs for the individual words weeks ago, but it was only last night that she and Becky had surprised him and taught him the special handshape.

Now, Sam and Becky each held one hand upright, their palms directed toward each other, fingers spread, the middle and ring fingers tucked down against their palms.

"I love you."

Kayla's eyes misted.

They turned, flashing their hands her way.

A tear trickled down her cheek. She returned the sign, then reached into her sleeve for the dainty hand-embroidered handkerchief Sharleen had delivered to her from Ellamae early that morning. A blue handkerchief, taking care of the something blue.

Sharleen had loaned Kayla a string of pearls to wear with her wedding dress.

The something old, they had decided, laughing, had to be four-year-old Becky.

And the double somethings new were, of course, the adoption papers and the marriage license Kayla had signed that morning.

Never would she have believed, when she'd driven up to Sam's ranch house just a few weeks ago, that she would become a wife and mother so soon afterward. And both on the very same day.

Becky kissed her daddy's cheek and ran out to join Ellamae and the judge on the dance floor.

Sam crossed the room to Kayla. "What's all this?" He reached up and brushed away a fresh tear.

She shook her head.

He chuckled. "If you can't get the words out, then sign them to me. We'll see if I can understand."

She simply raised her hand again, in the handshape she'd never let go.

He smiled. "Me, too." He signed the shortcut and touched his palm to hers. "And I promise you, whether I speak or sign those words, you can trust they will *always* be true."

"I don't have a doubt in the world about that, Sam."

The sudden gleam in his eyes told her she'd said exactly the right thing. Smiling, he raised his brows, touched the fingertips of one hand to his mouth, then brought all his fingertips together in front of him.

So she kissed him.

* * * * *

Harlequin®

COMING NEXT MONTH

Available June 14, 2011

#1357 THE MAVERICK'S REWARD
American Romance's Men of the West
Roxann Delaney

#1358 FALLING FOR THE NANNY
Safe Harbor Medical
Jacqueline Diamond

#1359 A COWGIRL'S SECRET
The Buckhorn Ranch
Laura Marie Altom

#1360 THE DADDY CATCH
Fatherhood
Leigh Duncan

You can find more information on upcoming
Harlequin® titles, free excerpts and more at
www.HarlequinInsideRomance.com.

REQUEST YOUR FREE BOOKS!
2 FREE NOVELS PLUS 2 FREE GIFTS!

LOVE, HOME & HAPPINESS

YES! Please send me 2 FREE Harlequin American Romance® novels and my 2 FREE gifts (gifts are worth about $10). After receiving them, if I don't wish to receive any more books, I can return the shipping statement marked "cancel." If I don't cancel, I will receive 4 brand-new novels every month and be billed just $4.24 per book in the U.S. or $4.99 per book in Canada. That's a saving of at least 15% off the cover price! It's quite a bargain! Shipping and handling is just 50¢ per book in the U.S. and 75¢ per book in Canada.* I understand that accepting the 2 free books and gifts places me under no obligation to buy anything. I can always return a shipment and cancel at any time. Even if I never buy another book, the two free books and gifts are mine to keep forever.

154/354 HDN FDKS

Name	(PLEASE PRINT)	
Address		Apt. #
City	State/Prov.	Zip/Postal Code

Signature (if under 18, a parent or guardian must sign)

Mail to the **Reader Service:**
IN U.S.A.: P.O. Box 1867, Buffalo, NY 14240-1867
IN CANADA: P.O. Box 609, Fort Erie, Ontario L2A 5X3

Not valid for current subscribers to Harlequin American Romance books.

Want to try two free books from another line?
Call 1-800-873-8635 or visit www.ReaderService.com.

* Terms and prices subject to change without notice. Prices do not include applicable taxes. Sales tax applicable in N.Y. Canadian residents will be charged applicable taxes. Offer not valid in Quebec. This offer is limited to one order per household. All orders subject to credit approval. Credit or debit balances in a customer's account(s) may be offset by any other outstanding balance owed by or to the customer. Please allow 4 to 6 weeks for delivery. Offer available while quantities last.

Your Privacy—The Reader Service is committed to protecting your privacy. Our Privacy Policy is available online at www.ReaderService.com or upon request from the Reader Service.

We make a portion of our mailing list available to reputable third parties that offer products we believe may interest you. If you prefer that we not exchange your name with third parties, or if you wish to clarify or modify your communication preferences, please visit us at www.ReaderService.com/consumerschoice or write to us at Reader Service Preference Service, P.O. Box 9062, Buffalo, NY 14269. Include your complete name and address.

HARI I

Harlequin® Blaze™ brings you
New York Times *and* USA TODAY *bestselling author*
Vicki Lewis Thompson with three new steamy titles
from the bestselling miniseries SONS OF CHANCE

Chance isn't just the last name of these rugged
Wyoming cowboys—it's their motto, too!

Read on for a sneak peek at the first title,
SHOULD'VE BEEN A COWBOY

Available June 2011 only from Harlequin® Blaze™.

"THANKS FOR NOT TURNING ON THE LIGHTS," Tyler said. "I'm a mess."

"Not in my book." Even in low light, Alex had a good view of her yellow shirt plastered to her body. It was all he could do not to reach for her, mud and all. But the next move needed to be hers, not his.

She slicked her wet hair back and squeezed some water out of the ends as she glanced upward. "I like the sound of the rain on a tin roof."

"Me, too."

She met his gaze briefly and looked away. "Where's the sink?"

"At the far end, beyond the last stall."

Tyler's running shoes squished as she walked down the aisle between the rows of stalls. She glanced sideways at Alex. "So how much of a cowboy are you these days? Do you ride the range and stuff?"

"I ride." He liked being able to say that. "Why?"

"Just wondered. Last summer, you were still a city boy. You even told me you weren't the cowboy type, but you're...different now."

He wasn't sure if that was a good thing or a bad thing. Maybe she preferred city boys to cowboys. "How am I different?"

"Well, you dress differently, and your hair's a little longer. Your face seems a little more chiseled, but maybe that's because of your hair. Also, there's something else, something harder to define, an attitude…"

"Are you saying I have an attitude?"

"Not in a bad way. It's more like a quiet confidence."

He was flattered, but still he had to laugh. "I just admitted a while ago that I have all kinds of doubts about this event tomorrow. That doesn't seem like quiet confidence to me."

"This isn't about your job, it's about…your…" She took a deep breath. "It's about your sex appeal, okay? I have no business talking about it, because it will only make me want to do things I shouldn't do." She started toward the end of the barn. "Now, where's that sink? We need to get cleaned up and go back to the house. Dinner is probably ready, and I—"

He spun her around and pulled her into his arms, mud and all. "Let's do those things." Then he kissed her, knowing that she would kiss him back, knowing that this time he would take that kiss where he wanted it to go. And she would let him.

Follow Tyler and Alex's wild adventures in
SHOULD'VE BEEN A COWBOY
Available June 2011 only from Harlequin® Blaze™
wherever books are sold.

™ Harlequin®

SPECIAL EDITION

Life, Love and Family

LOVE CAN BE FOUND IN THE MOST UNLIKELY PLACES, ESPECIALLY WHEN YOU'RE NOT LOOKING FOR IT...

Failed marriages, broken families and disappointment. Cecilia and Brandon have both been unlucky in love and life and are ripe for an intervention. Good thing Brandon's mother happens to stumble upon this matchmaking project. But will Brandon be able to open his eyes and get away from his busy career to see that all he needs is right there in front of him?

FIND OUT IN

WHAT THE SINGLE DAD WANTS...

BY *USA TODAY* BESTSELLING AUTHOR

MARIE FERRARELLA

AVAILABLE IN JUNE 2011
WHEREVER BOOKS ARE SOLD.